THE
WHITE
GERMAN
SHEPHERD

Also by Vicki Hearne

NERVOUS HORSES
IN THE ABSENCE OF HORSES
ADAM'S TASK: CALLING
ANIMALS BY NAME

THE
WHITE
GERMAN
SHEPHERD

a novel by
Vicki
Hearne

THE ATLANTIC MONTHLY PRESS
NEW YORK

This book is a work of fiction. The characters are figments of the author's imagination.

Published simultaneously in Canada
Printed in the United States of America
FIRST EDITION

Library of Congress Cataloging-in-Publication Data

Hearne, Vicki, 1946–
   The white German shepherd.
   1. Dogs—Fiction. I. Title.
PS3558.E2555W45   1988   813'.54   87-19536
ISBN 0-87113-196-X

Design by Laura Hough

The Atlantic Monthly Press
19 Union Square West
New York, NY 10003

First Printing

for my daughter,
Colleen Lerman,
and in honor of Gutenberg,
who was never wrong

A true-to-type German Shepherd Dog gives an impression of innate strength, intelligence and nimbleness. . . . His whole manner and behaviour should make it perfectly clear that he is sound in mind and body, and with the physical and intellectual attributes to make him always ready for tireless action as a working dog. He must have an abundance of temperament . . . innate nobility and alertness based on self-confidence . . . loyalty and incorruptibility. . . .

Full albinos . . . and . . . dogs with near-white coats but black noses—are alike to be firmly excluded from breed surveys and classification.

—From the Standard for the *Deutsche Schäferhunde*

I do not accept the bald statement "any dog which attempts to bite the judge must be disqualified" as a wise addition to the American Standard. A great deal depends upon the circumstances.

—M. B. Willis, B.Sc. Ph.D., *The German Shepherd Dog: Its History, Development and Genetics*

Contents

THE
WHITE
GERMAN
SHEPHERD

One
THE
COMMISSION

Sometimes, in Southern California, if you're a dog trainer, you go looking for a certain dog, and you have to do this knowing that maybe there isn't any such dog, although there's no reason why not. You probably have to do this every so often everywhere, for all sorts of reasons. But where Sam and I are trainers, Hollywood is just over the hill as distances go in California. Hollywood calls you up, even if you are in Tibet, and says they are looking for an Ibizan Hound that plays the harmonica and do you have one? And if you're me, you say, like a fool, that you do, and then you rush out and get an Ibizan and you spend the weekend teaching him to play the harmonica, and then you show up ready, you hope, for the turnabouts the director is going to pull, like he actually wanted a Pharaoh Hound, lots of white, and can you dye or bleach your Ibizan? Sometimes you can, sometimes not,

1

depends on the dog, and it can depend on a surprising number of other things.

This time what Hollywood—that is to say, in this case, Jack Kaye—wanted was a White German Shepherd, which is ridiculous. You don't look for a White German Shepherd when you need the steadiness a film dog has to have, and if you are me, you don't look for one at all, because what you want is a dog with substance, something bred to do a job and to stand with real feet planted on a real terrain—what the black-and-tans are bred for often enough so that you can find such dogs, but not *White* German Shepherds. They may have gotten better than when the story I am telling happened, but back then you could find a good one as easily as you could find snow in the Sahara Desert. They had no breed history in their feet, no meaning in their movements. Someone, as near as I could make out, had just started breeding the whites that were normally culled from the litter, so there were no real dogs, and if there had been, there was no tradition for them to plant their feet in. Dogs are like us, and there's more to us when we have a history.

"But maybe," Sam said one time when we had spent another week not finding anything, "if we find a good one, Hollywood will be the chance for the breed, and that will *be* something, working dogs made from, rather than pressed into service for, celluloid." Fat chance of that, of course, and Sam knows it.

Sam and I—Sam is Samuel Abraham Carraclough and I am Diane Brannigan—knew plenty about looking for dogs, and we were perfectly willing to use everything we knew to find this dog, including the fact that people don't automatically think of a 5'3", 100-pound woman when they think dog trainer.

Sam looks so much like a dog trainer that if he is in a room full of people with his best suit on and someone asks, "Which one is Sam?" and you say, "He's the dog trainer," they pick him out right away and usually jump back a little because they had been expecting Barbara Woodhouse. People aren't used to that much reality packed together like that. Sam used to be a ballet dancer, and when he moves, or doesn't move, it can slice right across your vision.

Sam would laugh at me while we were looking for the dog, saying, "Di, you are almost for real when you do your girl act," or some such remark. Sometimes he calls me Annie, and lately he adds, "It's a good cover, but you're overdoing it. You'll have to give it up, anyway, if you want Luke ever to notice who you are, and it's the only way for you to find out in time whether Luke is cotton candy all through, the way he looks."

Usually I would just say that I was so used to my cover that it would be strange now to go to any of the old disguises, or new ones, which was a lie. With Luke around, I had taken to changing my blouse around the kennel too. It wasn't a disguise, exactly. There were still times then when I thought I would someday know how to dress.

I didn't answer the part about Luke. "Cotton candy," to Sam, meant not to be trusted with the life of the kennel, and Luke was living at the kennel. It was true that I'd put some extra thought lately into the purchase of two blouses. Not shirts. And I was thinking of buying a skirt. Luke made me feel the gaiety of clothes, though I didn't know enough to do much about it. Sam was sharp about Luke, because until then there hadn't been anyone but me and Sam at the kennel—we hadn't agreed to keep our lovers out, but we just had for eight years—and Luke wasn't made of cotton candy, he just came from a different landscape.

Sometimes when people were mentally defective about dogs—there are more and more of them—thinking that dogs were pure and innocent, like typewriters, they would end up owning a good dog, anyway, and those were the ones who were put off by Sam, who, as I said, had never compromised with a dog and looked it, so when we were looking for a dog, I would make the calls, usually, and when it was one of those feather-brained breeders or their customers who think dog training is cruel, I'd wear a silk-blend blouse, hold my hands together and talk about being a woman living alone in the city. If Sam came with me, he would be a cousin or a boyfriend, just giving me a ride.

We wouldn't lie, but when people are talking about dogs, they are so eager for you to have the same idea in your head that they have in theirs, or else to be sure that you aren't smart enough to understand dogs the way they do, that you don't have to lie, and that goes double for scientists.

When we were looking for the Great Dane for Bob Cesneros, for example, I got a sudden notion and stuck my stomach out, so as to look even less like a cruel dog trainer, and the woman who was selling her dog and feeling guilty about it thought, "Nice young couple, she's pregnant," so she said that Danes were wonderful with children. And I said that I knew that, that I had read it in *The Complete Great Dane,* and Sam tried to look fatuously proud, the way he thought a father ought to look, and we bought that dog, who was a hell-raiser and not to be left alone with children. Not that he was mean, just too big and careless at eighteen months. A 165-pound puppy, too big and careless, which is why the woman was selling him. He was too rough for her and her children—he had dug holes in her carpet as well as the yard, but he was just what Cesneros wanted for the pilot for a TV series. He paid us well for him, and he still has him. He didn't get the contract for the series, but you'd be surprised how many perfume, automobile, detergent, and diaper commercials are improved by the presence of a Great Dane in the background, and anyway, what Bob wanted mostly was an excuse to own a spectacular dog. Bob's more of a tweed-coated hobo than a dog trainer, really. So the dog earns his keep, and Bob earns the dog.

As it happens, Sam and I aren't a nice young couple; neither of us could ever stand love songs and whatnot, we just can't figure out what to do with them (although Luke has a way of making me feel that I could). We were halfway to being in love before we noticed that and backed off, and just as well. We probably wouldn't be such good partners if we weren't both lousy lovers.

I don't mean, mind you, that Sam can't turn it on, and as for me, I can love a man up like nobody's business, just as long as I don't have to live with him, which is what's wrong with me. There is always something wrong with a dog trainer, and that's what it is with me, I'm too difficult for a man to live with, even if I didn't have more dogs than any man but Sam—who can't live with a woman—could put up with. So Sam and I make a good pair. We have two small houses at the kennel—we call it Neverland Kennel—with the dog runs between them. We share meals when neither of us has—I suppose I have to say, a date— and we get along like brother and sister. Better.

It turned out there was no need for Sam to play boyfriend or anything else while we were looking for the White German Shepherd because there wasn't a dog anywhere worth the trouble of a second look. Maybe Jouster—the dog came to us in the end, complete with that name—was looking for us, too, or how else would we have found him? I drove or flew to just about every kennel between Tijuana and Seattle, and we had a dog shipped in from Mexico City once, and another one from Dallas, Texas, and there wasn't a real dog anywhere. Not with the pigmentation and size old Jack Kaye wanted. The dogs were trash, every single one of them. No substance, no heart, no presence. I don't know what the people who breed these dogs are thinking of, and I don't want to know in case I get to feeling like forgiving them.

I said to Sam one day, coming away from a kennel, "I don't know! I don't know what the hell such people think they're doing!"

Sam said, "Maybe they're helping out the Ku Klux Klan," and that makes as much sense as anything. By their disguises shall ye know them.

Luke—Luke Zeller, with whom I am trying to live—said that Sam wasn't even a breeder, and why did this stuff cause him so much anxiety, and Sam said Luke didn't even begin to know what a good dog is.

And later on that day Luke said maybe I should think about living a little differently, get my hair styled, something a little elegant. This kind of thing had suddenly started coming from Luke when we started the search for the White Shepherd, and if it were any other man, I would have laughed at him for it, but it was *Luke*. Who didn't mean that he wanted me to be a decoration. Luke was saying it wistfully and trying to say something else that I didn't know about then, so I tried to answer, and what I said was that dogs were my only elegance. Only rich people have fireplaces in Jurupa, but Luke could make me think of life on the hearth, curled up like a cat, but that's what you do after everything else is done, and things weren't ever going to be done for me, there is always something to see to about the dogs. I didn't choose this life, it just turned out to be the life you lead if you start poor and have an eye and a heart for dogs. There's a tradition to such poverties—in my case, the Scotch-Irish who came over in the nineteenth century, leaving behind their bondage to the kennels and stables of royalty but bringing a dog or two, a horse, and in the dogs and horses, epic after epic in their genes.

You could get the wrong idea about Luke. Before Luke, I was with a man—he *didn't* live at the kennel—who made a virtue out of schlumping around drawing long faces about the state of things and calling it concern. He used to quote Milton where he wrote, "Hence, vain deluding joys!" and admired a book by Burton called *The Anatomy of Melancholy*. The way his temperament was, anything was okay as long as you saw the rain coming, including having the arrogance to be melancholy on other people's behalf. My behalf, for example, because I believed in heroic dogs, a "bankrupt idea," he said, and I wasn't getting rich, and I hadn't finished college, and what about my old age? It took me a while to figure out that my old age was my own concern and tell him to go bother someone else. A person like that, as good as he was at filling himself full of self-congratulation because he saw fly specks on everyone else's life, will do *anything*. There are people who are like fear-biting dogs, they're timid and they fool amateurs. But that was the first melancholy biter I ever knew.

Luke wasn't like that, but he was born to an idea of money, and now he had it, and he knew how expensive money was. What he didn't know was how expensive my poverty was, how I had no choice about paying what I paid for it, didn't want a choice, even though until Luke it had cost me my love life, and at the moment I don't mean sex and emotional folderol.

"I can't *afford* to have my hair styled," I said another time, and neither of us were saying what we meant, so he thought I was too proud to take the money from him, as if I had been talking about cash. No amount of cash was going to change the demands I found in the world. Sam and I have trained plenty of dogs *for* people with money, and that's well and good and as it should be. Money buys dog training, of course, but you can't train dogs *with* that kind of money, the kind that changes the shape of your vocal cords. It's not a matter of there being anything wrong with money, it's a matter of landscapes.

Luke knows that, and I've said it wrong, because Luke *did* know how expensive the kennel was. He talked about his writing and the training together, and he knew what *expensive* was. And the way he had of looking around him and *seeing* so much, that had to have been expensive. But he was backed off, I didn't know what by, but he no longer wanted writing to be that expensive.

Another time, when the three of us were having coffee, Luke turned out to think that the point of the movie for me and Sam was money. The idea of the big break was part of it, of course, but that wasn't it, and even with the help of the Teamsters—you have to be a union member to work an animal on a set—we didn't expect money.

Luke said, "If you get a good contract and the movie goes

big, maybe you could quit having to teach and train six days a week plus Sundays, only train the dogs you want to train." Sam was there, so Luke couldn't say the rest. He wanted more time with me, and he wanted us to be able to go on trips together, and like I said, I wanted that kind of thing, too, with Luke, because Luke had eyes that could take in revolutions and mountains without strain, so I could probably go away with Luke without going *away*, but there was always something more to do about the dogs, I couldn't seem to plan it, and now there was the White German Shepherd and the movie.

Sam looked at me with that gaze of his, and I knew what he was thinking and was hoping he wouldn't say it because Luke meant well, he just had no way of knowing how long Sam and I had spent being the way we were, and I'm not saying the kennel didn't get to be a chore, and the classes, but there wasn't another life in which you could see what we saw every day, miracles as homely as milk, and Sam looked at me longish and then said to Luke, gently enough, "This isn't a hobby, you know."

Luke said, "Yes, I know. I'm sorry." His face shone with calm and thought. It does that, and Luke knows when he's in the presence of something, which was why he had been the kind of writer he was; most people brought their dogs for training the way they brought their cars for a lube, and that wasn't Luke, but Luke had an impatience that would attack him, especially now, and his impatience was leery and kept asking what and why, and *that* I couldn't say no matter how much I talked.

Training Prince hadn't been a vocation for Luke, but it hadn't been a hobby, either. He was married once, and after his wife died, he had just folded up, spent three years in grief. Fortunately for Luke he had had the dog, and in the course of writing his features about Freddie, he had found out about our classes and brought Prince for training. At first, like a lot of people, he had gone through the exercises the way you follow assembly directions, but you can't give a command and get a real response and stay locked up in grief—Luke couldn't, anyway. Prince and the training class had tricked him into love, and then he had loved me. That's what obedience does for some people; they go stumbling through a class, through the motions of love, and then they stumble into the real thing with their dogs at heel.

Luke had said it when it happened, having coffee with me after the class in which it happened. "I had fumbled my way through your instructions, hooking up the light line, then making the big fuss you said to make about unhooking the leash and tossing it away, and I set off at heel, and dammit! Prince stayed right with me, so I suddenly had to think about what had been keeping him at heel all along. I thought it had been the leash doing it, but it had been the dog and I doing it."

Luke was right—the leash was just a detail, training was love, but there was something deeper yet, something less personal. Most people didn't see as much as Luke saw, not on their first dogs, not as sharply as Luke saw it, that it isn't the *equipment* that keeps the dogs at heel; talking with Luke while he was discovering this was how I fell in love with him. But there is the something deeper that may be love, too, if love is awe without morality. I would say that to Luke when I began to trust him, and he said that Sam and I were nothing *but* morality, taking care of dogs and helping people with their dogs all the time, so there is more than one sense of morality, or else Luke was wrong, but he wasn't. I said, "Okay, but then morality is just one of the details, like training equipment. It's for something else." Luke was spooked by this something else. He mentioned the Spanish Inquisition once, but you mustn't judge him by that, because he would say things by way of exploring an idea, and that time he went on and said, "Of course, the Inquisitors probably weren't doing it for God at all. I met a man who seemed genuinely to fit the description 'a man of God,' and he knew how to let the world alone."

Sometimes I think that maybe I was trying to talk about God, except when I heard other people talk about God. There's a way the light gets more real than anything, I see it mostly in the movements of certain dogs, all dogs but certain dogs especially, but you see it in paintings, too, or I used to when I wanted to paint. The light gets real, and for the sake of that light, training dogs is a matter of twenty-seven hours a day and expensive. Luke said it made him nervous when I tried to talk about that, but Sam has seen it, sees it all the time. It has given him a Look; he's always listening. And Sam and I kept looking for the White German Shepherd.

I don't know breeding all that well, just training, but anybody who hasn't sold his soul to Sweetheart Dog Cologne would breed better dogs than what we saw, even if he did have his head full of crazy ideas about "type." That's what the breeders talk about instead of talking about dogs. They talk about type, and they get a disgusting, righteous, imitation mystical look in their eyes when they talk about a "typy" dog, just as though they were talking about something real, a dog that could do a job of work for you. A dog with a heart that can get broken, so you have to remember not to break your own heart, although there are some dogs who will take God as their elegance.

Of course, there really is such a thing as type, but if you take care of your work, type will take care of itself. I mean, if you've got sheep, you don't breed the pups that run your sheep off a cliff; that's how you end up with sheepdogs, and God takes care of the rest. A human being can't fully see a dog, really, all we can do is work them and know them that way, so there is always something else to see to.

Two
JACK
KAYE

I should have started by telling you about Jack Kaye, who is, or was, a Big Name—trained a fair number of the dogs you have come to know and love on your movie and television screens. You may not have heard of him because he hasn't done much for a while, but he decided to make a comeback. No one but people like me and Sam knew this, because Kaye was finally afraid that he couldn't make it any longer. None of us wanted this news spread around; it made us feel wobbly, and I forbade Freddie Kubie, our kennel hand, to go with us, plead as Freddie would and did about wanting to show his Bluetick off to Kaye. Freddie has red hair, freckles, and acts like a comic version of some kid in one of those old dog stories, who has single-minded dedication—before he finds out about the bad guys in the dog world. What Freddie did was to teach Blue, his Bluetick Coonhound, to open

11

elevators and select the right floor. I don't know how he did it. Kaye was getting old, and he hadn't done more than one or two commercials for years, just lived with a couple of dogs his chauffeur groomed for him, spilling expensive booze on his four-hundred-dollar jackets—he could afford to. Everybody knew what he'd done. And then he decided he would show the world he was still The Man, that he could still train a dog—his way. But he was not really up to, or interested in, chasing around the country looking for dogs. And why should he when he could pay me and Sam to do it?

He wanted the White German Shepherd in order to do a kind of remake of *The Call of the Wild,* and it was going to be good, too, a real dog movie. The dog had to be pure white, not biscuit, with a coal-black nose and the eyes just right. No pink noses, nothing. Everything just right. And he wanted me and Sam, either or both of us, to put a certain kind of training on the dog—the standard routines, climb things, snarl, bark, head down and pretend to sleep, jump, retrieve, pull a sled, look back over his left shoulder, pretend to love an actor when an actor isn't, from a dog's point of view, a person at all.

Anyway, Kaye—and he was a Grand Old Man, too, no matter what I say about him—called us up about finding the dog for him. Summoned us to a hotel suite at the Beverly Hilton the size of three full-scale kennels. He had a dog with him, Pierre, the big clownish Bouvier you all know from that movie about Arkansas, the dog who gets wounded by the spooky city slicker who thinks the dog is a bear. I still don't know what the point of the hotel suite was, except that Kaye can afford it, and some dog trainers are like children with extra money. It was as far from our kennel in Jurupa as it was from his house in La Jolla. But maybe he had business in Los Angeles. There is no point, usually, in trying to figure out a dog trainer who isn't actually working a dog.

So there was Kaye, a big man with some of his pre-alcoholic

dignity still about him, in that huge piece of empty luxury that couldn't give it back to him, and he started right out by telling us what he didn't want in the way of training. You'd think that a dog trainer would have learned what the chances are of reforming another dog trainer, but Kaye hadn't learned that, or else he had temporarily forgotten it, so he told us a lot, walking in figure eights and funny squares around the room, imitating a robot, which is what he didn't want.

It is almost but not quite possible to turn a dog into a robot. Precision in a dog's work no more destroys his personality than it destroys a dancer's grace, no more than cell structure destroys the suppleness of a leaf or a dog, and dog training is an art, not a social occasion, you have to mean everything you say and there are no compromises.

But that's as far as I ever get, trying to explain it to people. Either you know or you don't know. If you know, there's no need to talk about it, and if you don't know, there is no way to talk about it. Except that Sam and I do talk about it, finding new ways to say it to each other, as though we had to relearn dog training every morning.

I liked Kaye and wanted to say it to him. He hadn't taught classes in forty years and had forgotten—not about his dogs, but about other dogs, about anything but his way, and we couldn't really talk dogs. Usually you can't, not with anyone.

Sam and I know, but how can I know whether or not anyone else's knowledge is fraudulent or not? Especially Luke, because in the kennel itself, respect wasn't enough, Luke had that and no mistake, but his impatience wasn't going to leave him alone, or me, so he would just have to know. He would, I thought; his eyes were good enough, if I could show him.

This began getting urgent about right here, about the time we first visited Kaye, because this was where I let Luke sort of half move in at the kennel.

Sam and I say things, especially me, because things need to

get said even though you can't say much, which doesn't always matter, except when you really have something to say, when there needs to be more room in the world for something.

But we don't say anything to Kaye, I should get back to Kaye, and Malibu. I wander when I think of Luke. I was thinking of his eyes. Kaye is doing a wonderful imitation of no dog you ever saw or ever will see outside of a cartoon version of a behaviorist's dream of machinery.

But then he showed Pierre off to us, and the dog could do routines so it would take your breath away. Kaye is a grand old man, make no mistake. Pierre worked with disciplined glee. Snatched my jacket and hid it under the couch, then pretended to find it and return it to me, started to lift a leg on Kaye, then switched to scratching his left ear, fetched a bottle of Jack Daniel's, green label, picking it out from the twenty or so bottles on the bar, went back and got the ice bucket, ran to the door and snarled as if he smelled a mildew of spies.

Then he stole the covers and the pillow from the bed and covered himself up, lying still with only the gleam from a happy, conceited eye to show he wasn't sleeping innocently. After that he got up and howled as mournfully as you please, straining a little to get the proper mellowness into his voice, which was by nature somewhat gravelly and deep. Opera is nothing to what that dog could make in the way of grieving melodies.

When he's working a dog—when he used to work dogs, I should say—Kaye was on top of the dog every second, snapping his fingers, turning, talking, urging with his very earlobes. His thing is to get a puppy and live with it, working twenty-seven hours a day for as much as two years. It's not much use in real life, this "training"—at least not if you want a dog who can work for you even when you forget the Liver Snaps, or if you have a broken leg or something—but it is wonderful, anyway, and maybe Kaye just uses food rewards on television and not when he's doing honest work.

But now things had come around. What Kaye was hiring

Sam and me to do was to put the training on the dog he wanted for this movie. And what he wanted, what he had to have, was a full-grown White German Shepherd with heart and presence, and he didn't have two to three years this time, and not much health. He knew as well as me and Sam that food rewards and kitchy-koo don't always work so well on ninety pounds of adult dog who already has opinions and his own life-style worked out.

Sam and I didn't have to discuss accepting the commission, I guess, but we had a few things that needed going over, so we withdrew for a private chat, downstairs in the coffee shop of the hotel.

Kaye hadn't said on the phone, or else we couldn't imagine him saying and therefore didn't hear him say, that it would be easier to find a miniature polar bear somewhere in Florida than a solid-white German Shepherd; the dogs are not bred for work and haven't any presence or substance, though, again, there's no reason they couldn't, but they don't. Anyway, white is not a good color on the kind of coat a Shepherd has, although the coat could be spruced up cosmetically, but that didn't help our searching problem, which was: How were we going to find a good White German Shepherd when the phrase was practically a contradiction in terms? From our point of view, at least.

There were also the worries Sam voiced when I was done with my tirade, and Sam growled a little.

"Are you sure that Kaye has still got it? That stuff on that Bouvier, I'd guess that was about 3,728 bottles of Jack Daniel's, green label, in the past."

But I had started a hard-edged dream, one you could work for, and said, "Sam. Maybe this is a real break, and if it isn't, what can we lose?" The break didn't mean money, as I've said— it meant wanting something large. What can you lose?

Sam—how do I explain Sam? Sam was fearless because he had seen grief through to its bottom and been devoured, and if you're already devoured, Hollywood isn't going to get so much as a nibble at your soul, but that also meant he knew about consequences. I once saw Nijinsky dance, on a friend's television set, and even on the tube you could see the way Nijinsky's vision reorganized the space and time he moved in. Sam had wanted to be a ballet dancer when he was younger—it was Sam who had made me see Nijinsky—and he trained and taught the way he danced, rechoreographing the air around him, like a sculptor's chisel. Changing the equations of space. So Sam knew what happens when you go to do that and nothing happens, when you dance with everything you've got and nothing happens except that space and time collapse in a jumble of rags on top of you. To look for and to train this dog would be to dance with everything we had, not for a client, not for a job of work, not to have a dog ourselves, but for a movie. What did we have to lose?

Plenty, of course, if you're sensible enough to be superstitious in the right way, as Sam said afterward. We were sitting in a trucker's restaurant, trying to get the smell of the Hilton out of our noses, that odorless odor that destroys tracking dogs. Sam got up to get coffee, and I looked around at the truckers, noticing that there were some changes lately in the patterns you see in these restaurants; patterns of faces. It used to be about a third of the guys who came through a truck stop were genial-looking toughs. I mean, they were toughs, but it was health and hope and love that made them that way. Then you'd see some who were a bit younger, who were just finding out what the pressure to get a semi from Denver to San Diego in twenty-four hours or under can do to you, finding out that it is only one person or another that can be fair, not the world, and their eyes jumped from frustration and Dexedrine, but if you hung out for a few years in that restaurant, you had small conversations with the same guys coming through, and they became healthier most of the time. Despite the pieties of a therapy-sick culture, some of them used their own hearts and imaginations to get off the drugs or the booze or the womanizing, reinventing the landscapes of their lives as they drove through them. Some of them talked pretty violent, some didn't. Some would tell you about the new quarterhorse stud, or the new wife, or the new kid or the new house they'd gotten since they last saw you, and they all had dreams, almost all of them, and looked alive. Undesirable, maybe, but alive.

Now I was wondering where this new look most of them had came from, a grayness, as though nothing could matter again, ever. In the young ones as well as the old ones.

That's why the movie mattered, I thought, because there has to be something in the world that matters, and that's what a dog story is about.

Sam said, "We find a dog, they do this movie, maybe the dog will have something to say to these guys. Doesn't look like anyone else is talking to them." Sam wasn't talking about saving their souls, or the world. He just thought they looked like they needed a good dog.

Sam had taught a dance class in a prison once, and he had said that at first he couldn't get anyone to move. Then he had said he had realized that they were in prison, of course they weren't moving. So he had invented formal movements in a space no more than twelve inches from their bodies, then eighteen inches, and the men started moving. He had them dancing in their cells, he had said. He was around the prison in the first place, of course, because he was supervising the security dogs there.

Sam went on, looking around the restaurant. "It looks like people need more space to move around in, people can't move, and if they like dogs, they can't move because they don't know what's going on with dogs." Sam's a dreamer. But he taught dance in a prison. Dog training too. The way Sam did it, teaching dog training, it was like teaching dance. Clearing space with a chisel. Recarving the equations.

He had some coffee and said, "People come into our classes like these guys, jerky, tentative, closed up—like if they made a real move with their dogs, they'd crash into a stone wall. The movie could show what scope is, what the scope of a dog is."

But there was still the problem of this ridiculous search Kaye had sent us on, and he knew better—this business of coming up with a White German Shepherd who could do the job.

Sam said, "We'll be okay, so long as we don't let it matter, about the break."

There were enough problems, including the fact that Kaye had gotten it into his head that the part called for some clowning, and you don't start right off with a German Shepherd of any color if you want clown scenes on camera.

Okay, that matters, too, not letting the Big Break matter, if you want to be a real dog trainer, otherwise you spend the first half of your life waiting for it and the second half bitter because it never happened.

Sam didn't get to looking like a nimble chunk of granite by dreaming about angels descending with movie contracts in their hands, so what Sam says and what I say is that we're just finding another dog for another client. Everything else is time, and like the cowboy said, time takes care of itself, you just leave time alone. That's exactly what Luke said that evening, in what he seems to have thought of as an effort to comfort and calm me, but I hadn't needed calming. Luke likes to think slowly, always, like his pipe smoke, circling around, and so do I sometimes, but now it was time to think with an edge, and long, slow thinking isn't what calms me, it gets fuzzy, not so much when Luke does it, though. I was in a mood for edges. What calms me is dogs working, mostly.

Kaye had told us, after he got through with the part about Jack Kaye being the one dog trainer in the whole world with enough finesse and spirit really to handle a movie dog, that the film was going to show everyone what dog training is. What it is, what a dog is, and it sounded half the time as though Kaye—Jack Daniel's or no—would be in a position to do it, he was going to be a kind of codirector, and even if he couldn't train the way

Sam could, he could believe in the flame of a dog's heart, which is what dog training is in service of.

Which is not quite the way Jack London has it, with the dealer clubbing the dog a dozen times. Any dog you have to club that many times, you probably aren't going to win with, especially if you think you can train a dog with a club. There's a difference between the kind of respect a club creates and the kind love does, and chances are the dog isn't going to be able, much less willing, to pull for you the way Buck pulls for John Thornton, a thousand-pound sled, its runners frozen to the ground, but that's the way it is in that story, the truth blown up so high and turned so far upside down that it becomes the truth again, and this is the way it was even in the movie they already made, with a St. Bernard playing Buck.

Dog training is, at some point near its center, brutal and always ruthless, but not physically—it's not cruelty I'm talking about, although there are people who are cruel to dogs. This has nothing to do with cruelty, it's just the impersonal logic of the thing. You just have to clear your mind and body, and the dog's mind and body, of all extraneous postures, and it is, in time, a little bit as though the dog forgave you, but what gets forgiven is the nature of things, and it's not the dogs who forgive that.

Luke gets stiff and looks ready to leave the room when I talk this way. But he doesn't leave. He says he panics, and his panic says it sounds a bit like a kind of classical, platonic Fascism. He says this gently, wanting to instruct me, because he had seen things, and he really has seen things, you can see it in his eyes, Luke's eyes look around him, seeing more, and like eyes that have really seen things, his eyes have strength in them and no harm, but he panics in his talk sometimes. I say that it's just dog training. I get impatient, too, and one time I was griping because the AKC gives breed championships without a training test, they were ruining dogs, and he wanted to know what I had against the AKC and trotted out the argument I sometimes use on him, which is that, okay, there's plenty wrong with the AKC, but the thing about money and institutional prestige is that they can do good things in spite the people who own them.

I don't always talk this way.

Sam says, absently, in the truck stop. *"The Call of the Wild* is not about the submission of dogs," and it will matter whether or not the moviemakers know this. A good dog, of course, will sometimes chew on people or behave in a generally antisocial fashion, because the better a dog is, the stronger he feels it when the posture is wrong, the less agreeable the dog is to submitting to the wrong posture, and sometimes you do lay into a good dog by way of saying, "I know better than this." Not very often, of course, because it's not very often anyone knows something better than anything, people do the best they can, but there ought to be a movie about the way the landscape comes around sometimes, and honors the dog's presence in it.

A quality White German Shepherd. I don't know if there can be such a thing, but if there was, you could dream it up this way:

Say a White German Shepherd, standing by your side, so that you and the dog are both looking ahead, in snow as white as the dog, and there is, for the moment, no Gap. The Gap is everywhere, between lovers, between friends, between the world and God, between the mind and what you say. In dog training you go for the right posture, ruthlessly, and then there is no Gap, things fit together, and when they fit, they move. A real dog movie, with the right dog in it, would show that: that things can fit, they can move, even without the evening news. So now, in that truck stop, it matters something god-awful to me and Sam whether or not this movie ever gets made, which is why Sam is edgy as he hunches up around himself like a Bull Terrier that's worried, and says, "We don't know."

"Yeah, Sam, but if they pay just a little bit of attention, if even just the cameraman himself pays attention, makes people see the white dog in the white snow, and maybe the man's face is dirty in the right way, and it ought to be someone who could play a deaf-mute, it's the same thing."

Sam says, "It's hard to see white on white. But . . . if we can find the right dog . . ." We get up from the Formica table, pay, wonder about the visions of the truck drivers and drive back to Jurupa, in a state of innocence, with no idea at all what looking for that dog was going to mean.

Our kennel used to be pretty standard, but by the time this story began happening, we had Freddie, a funny, skinny kid, and his two dogs, and maybe it was Freddie Kubie who started it all by doing such a good job with his Bluetick Coonhound, Blue, who got to be enough of a local character so that Luke's editor got interested and sent him to write about Blue and Freddie. Freddie has enthusiasm the way the sun has light, and like I said, even when Luke had just about given up on everything, Freddie got him to come out of his desert refuge and train Prince. Freddie will start thinking that it would be fun to have some different-looking obstacles for the dogs to jump, and then he's out in the orange groves finding still usable wood in tumbledown shacks and talking me out of the dog trailer to haul it with. We've got a picket-fence jump, painted green, blue, and yellow; a jump painted like a stone wall; and one with six striped bars. Freddie got the idea from watching the Olympic horses jumping. That's the way it's going to be around Freddie—Freddie will start thinking, and then things are a little odd and more colorful.

It was a White German Shepherd we were looking for, a proper dog, a particular white, but the universe makes fun of you sometimes. Or so it seemed one morning when: There George was, fluffy and white and contrary and only semi-loyal, the way the Nordic breeds are—and George is witty in the bargain—and there was nothing at all reasonable about an intelligent young man who had the experience of a fine working Coonhound suddenly possessing, and possessing while inhabiting my kennel, a Samoyed.

"Why in the world a Samoyed?" I asked Freddie.

Freddie just looked as happy as his goofball dog. "Isn't he beautiful?" he said. "A Coonhound isn't everything." He then produced a red, white and blue dumbell and tossed it for George, who retrieved it with some nonregulation bounces, and added, "Besides, that big white coat, it looks nice and gaudy when he goes over the jumps I painted."

Sam said, "Well, this isn't the sort of thing I'd think of, but it doesn't hurt this place to have somebody thinking a little fancy."

So Freddie brought his changes with him, thinking fancy. There was already change, in old Kaye's calling us up and letting us in on the movie, but change brings the need for more change, and maybe we were going to need a witty Samoyed; you never know.

Three

LUKE AND
SAM AT
RIGHT
ANGLES

Most of our money, despite the boarding and training, comes from the classes we teach, mainly in Novice Obedience. People learn to say, "Sit," "Stay," "Down," "Stand," "Heel," and "Come" to their dogs, and they learn to do this off-lead. Put another way: They learn how to walk and talk in a straight line with their dogs at heel.

They and their dogs learn trust. It's a funny species, human being, that has to take a class in how to hang around with a dog, but hanging around with a dog is more complicated than you might suppose, and it's mostly not written down anywhere. One of the things you have to learn is how to do nothing industriously, and I don't mean transcendental meditation. Another thing I don't mean is boot camp. The problem is that human beings have lost the authority of stillness—maybe it's Adam and

Eve's fault—and since dogs hang out with us, they need some clarifying too. So when an owner gets dedicated to actually getting a sit out of Fido, and right now, instead of burbling, "Sit, sit, sit," all day long, they also start paying attention to Fido, get dedicated to the dog and then they've earned some authority again. But you have to learn stillness, or else you don't know action. One command. Fido might be a quarter of a mile away, paying court to royal rabbits, and then he's there, in front of you, as square as carpentry. *One* command.

The classes were five nights a week and twice on Saturdays. This was the good old days I'm talking about here, before the parks became free-fire zones between the cops and the thugs, and the thugs, some of them, were young enough to have less of an idea of consequences than a four-month-old Irish Setter, puppies with knives, so the classes were in public parks and recreation areas, out in the open, no fences, or else at our kennel. Our clients come from the whole of the tri-county area, plus L.A.

Nowadays the classes can't be genuinely public. They're even indoors when we can transport the mats to keep the dogs from getting injured. They are at a local Y or behind some very secure chain-link fencing, but I am talking about something earlier, when citizenship, good or bad, wasn't on the run.

In the Tuesday night class, which was the one at our kennel, out in the pasture we had seeded for a training area, Luke appeared. The first night of our classes, people are supposed to come without their dogs, so it was just Luke, lounging about real quiet, smoking a pipe. He slouched, but he slouched in an efficient way, like a hound dog all hunkered down on haunches and forepaws, quiet for his heart and lungs to get rested so he's ready when it is time to be ready. Luke looks casual and quiet, but so does a sequoia, and a sequoia has roots that go out and register everything. Some sequoias know when a rabbit goes by a hundred feet from the trunk.

He had a good little Shetland Sheepdog named Prince, and

the reason a long, rangy, thinking type like Luke had a quick, sharp-turning, prancing dog like a Sheltie was because he used to have a wife, Esther, and she died of cancer. While she was dying, Luke bought Prince for her. Not that they didn't have dogs. They had a cattle ranch and they had plenty of dogs, but they were cattle dogs, too big and rough for Esther when she got so weak.

Esther died, and Luke still had Prince, and Luke told me, which I could guess from meeting Prince, that the dog had been just right—light enough to jump on her bed without distressing her when she called him, with quick, soft ways of touching her, Luke said. Prince would put out a paw to touch her arm like a consolation, delicate as a cat, with those white forepaws so lovely that sometimes they seemed to shed whiteness into the air like health.

Esther is also one of the reasons I've got to be careful about thinking too much about Luke. I don't mean that he still loves her; it's several years now since she died, but Luke keeps saying, apropos of nothing in particular, *never again,* which means that he does still somehow love her, so he says that, the way people do when their dogs die, right after they die, not wanting to be at hazard again.

With her dead, he sold the ranch to the foreman, who'd been saving to buy his own place. He came to inland Southern California, the desert part, bought a little cabin up in Oak Glen, all so as never to have anything at stake again. Of course, training a dog is putting yourself at stake, but people don't usually know that until it's too late, and there's no way out but straight through, or a falling away from the heart.

Sometimes when I talked about how people would *know* if we found the dog and the movie got made, he would talk about the times when, as he put it, everyone in America, or so it seemed to him, was ready to put him or herself at stake: there was that much heart in this country, and Luke had been one of the people putting himself at stake. Not anymore, he would say to me, emphatically and more than once. "No more quests and causes," he would say, making me nervous.

He was one of the people who, in the sixties, created a kind of journalism that makes writing into an action instead of a piece of duty and decorum. Or else he made action into a kind of decorum, the same thing in him that made him do such a good job with Prince when Prince was his first dog. I don't mean there's no duty and decorum in Luke—that was going to be my problem, worrying about Luke and decorum—but then Luke put everything, including the safeguards of his own sanity, second to writing, writing, writing. That was before Esther, when everything could be put at risk. He told me these things almost as if he were talking about morally neutral events, his voice unnaturally even most of the time, as when you say, thinking about something else, "It's raining," "There's a new kind of Cheer out," or, "I put everything at risk."

That's the way he said it, but I found later that he had kept pictures of himself, which he showed to me, urging courage and revolution to blacks, to everyone who had a raw deal almost, in corners of Idaho and then at Berkeley, when he was still a student. I've seen some of his writing in *The New Republic* and *Rolling Stone,* and even now, with the dust of going on a decade and a half on them, even now you can read what he wrote and know that there was a full-sized flesh-and-blood human being moving in concert with those words, and in them.

He doesn't do that anymore. When Esther died, he hung on around the ranch for a while, but Esther, he found, had been the point of the ranch for him. For all he is so solitary—polite enough to people and talkative enough with me, but solitary—he is not one for getting his jollies from loveless achievements, so he sold the ranch, and there was enough money from it, even after he took care of Esther's niece's graduate school expenses and gave her a grubstake, to provide him with an income. Not wealth, but he could survive, and that's about all he was willing to do, he says, so he moved down here, got the little place in Oak Glen.

Now he writes about things like the Willie Boy monument up in the high desert. It used to be you could reach it by car, but a storm took care of that, grabbed the road right off the mountain, and the monument isn't even where Willie Boy is really buried, the Indians say, and so does Luke. And Luke writes about the latest search for the Peg Leg Pete mine, about the old desert rats who guard the tortoises in Tortoise Valley with shotguns. He writes about the eerily lovely hieroglyphics.

Will, the managing editor of the *Jurupa Herald*, told me he couldn't figure it; Luke ought to be running *The Washington Post* or something by now, he said; he's not one of those half-baked dreamers who don't write about politics because they haven't the muscle for it, but Will says cheerfully that the *Herald* is happy enough to "exploit" him; he writes rings around everyone in his features. Will says he's got enough scope to handle any story on any newspaper, and I can see that. He can write so that a story about the wrangler in Twentynine Palms who still uses the saddle the sheriff used in the 1909 manhunt has enough significance to include Paris and Bombay, the way van Gogh did with an old shoe.

The story about the Palm Springs land rip-off from the Indians, the one the *Herald* got the Pulitzer Prize for a while back, opened up again in a fresh way, and Will wanted Luke on that story—there really are still a few of the old-style loyal-opposition-type rabble-rousers on the paper, but Luke wouldn't do it. I asked him why not.

"Yeah, here's what will happen," he said. "I start talking to Indians, they start finding out about things like the Constitution, about human rights, about how to reason, and they get ideas about law school for themselves so they can help their people, but all that happens is that undergraduate school at Berkeley, or UCLA or wherever, is confusion, so after a while you've got a bitter, incurably resentful Indian. Of course, if the Indian stays on the reservation, you've still got a bitter, resentful Indian—drunk, too—but it won't be quite such a full and detailed resentment. Years of false hope makes bitterness that much worse—for the Indians, at least."

I didn't believe this and was surprised to hear it from Luke, even though his voice wasn't disillusioned and tired but, the way his words sound here, just matter-of-fact. I didn't know that the typewriter had conspired with a stray bit of history and turned itself around on him with a vengeance. I said that what people needed to learn was that things outside of themselves can *matter*. A hopeless quester, Luke called me tenderly enough, adding that one had to get over quests. I was to hear more of that sort of thing from Luke, but then I wasn't used to it, and I thought I could say that surely finding out about things like the Constitution was worthwhile, and the Indians didn't belong to Luke, but writing did, and the Constitution and some other things belonged to the Indians.

That day a guy had come by in a Mercedes—I've got nothing against Mercedes, but their drivers are more likely than not to talk funny—asking about training for his Ridgeback. A Ridgeback needs remedial work the day it's born. "But won't it hurt him?" the owner simpered. The sort of owner who won't harm a hair on the dog's head until the dog gets inconvenient and worse, and then sends the dog to the pound, or to the vet to be put to sleep on the advice of a "pet therapist."

"Goddamn right," Sam said, "it'll hurt, and it'll give him the only freedom that's worth a damn, the freedom of insight and the right to meaningful action."

I was going to tell Luke about that, but then he started talking about the Crusades and all of the fantods and bloodshed that went into that, and I had already once gotten almost fatally confused by one man who went on about Shakespeare's trage-dies, so Luke was part of why I was going to drive around California for a while, with my Wolfhound Homer, looking for the dog for Kaye, trying to think of something besides Luke. I couldn't not love Luke, couldn't be around him and be unaware of the translucent knowledge in his movements, also couldn't forget his hesitations about the kennel, the search, the movie.

The other man, the who who talked about the moral perfections of melancholy and the bankruptcy of heroism, had a way of frowning piously like a Methodist preacher, but try telling one hundred and seventy pounds of Irish Wolfhound about the wonders of melancholy. Homer just doesn't respond to me when I'm thinking about that, or about that guy.

There was some of that in Luke, but it wasn't so deep, or so I was betting. He just happened to be down rather than actively studying melancholy, but he's been low and almost out once in a while for three years or more now. And he has *reasons*, arguments, steps in logic to justify it all. There's something in here about what a private, idiosyncratic thing logic can be. It's not necessarily the impersonal bit about unarguable axioms you get the idea it is, not for dog trainers. I mean, *whose axioms?*

I dug a hole in hard ground on a hot day for a Great Dane three years ago, my dog Duke, who carried children on his back at the children's hospital, and who once, when Sam did a brief stint as a rodeo clown, had the courage to run interference between Brahman bulls and fallen riders. Carrying children and thinking about them, and fending off insane bulls, in a dog like Duke, it comes from the same place. So I am in a position to know that grief and death, the physical part, can be as ephemeral as everything else. With corpses—well, on the edges of the desert, even if you don't bury a corpse, the ants have turned it into flowers within three months. The only time the smell stays around is when you think you've got to throw your heart into the grave with the corpse. That's the grave-side temptation. Don't. A handful of dust will do, and it's cleaner, but a discarded heart smells for quite some time.

When my dog, Duke, the Great Dane, died, I had to console the *vet*, that's what kind of dog Duke was. I bought I don't know how many Scotches for that vet, and he's a Seventh Day Adventist.

One evening Luke and Sam and I were having dinner outside—it was hot but it was the time of day when it was hotter in the house. Sam made a mess of fried chicken, and Luke made spinach salad and heated rolls. While Sam cooked, he talked about how misguided it was just to have cold food in the summer—fried chicken was his idea, based on his fantasy notion that hot cooking like that puts you in touch with summer, which is why fried chicken was deeply part of the Deep South. This nonsense was fine with me, so long as it was Sam's kitchen that was turning into an oven. Sam knew a bit about the South from having been on the Tensas Swamp in Louisiana, learning about hog dogs, and had learned there how to tell stories about everything, even fried chicken.

Though it had been cooling off a little, it was still hot enough that Homer was snuggled up in the pit he had dug for himself around the roots of the eucalyptus tree. Twice while we were eating, he took off on his self-appointed rounds, checking every fence, every bit of brush, the welfare of the neighbor's milk goat, and the land around the house and runs. Luke hadn't seen Homer do this yet, not at dusk, and became almost mellow. Wolfhounds aren't sentry dogs, but they aren't dumb, either, and this part of Jurupa is rough enough that Homer keeps a wide and accurate eye on the house, kennels and grounds, and the dogs don't bark at him when he comes by. Instead, each one exchanges a brief sniff through the chain link with him, touching bases. I was watching Homer, so I don't remember clearly how it came about that Sam was talking.

He was, though, and there was Luke, pushing his tomatoes around and Sam telling about Zeus, the dog he had in Vietnam. Luke got curiously antagonistic to the story, and Sam was angry, telling his story like a cautionary tale, except it wasn't clear what Luke was being cautioned about, except maybe the fact that Sam might just decide to tell one of his hard-edged yarns if it felt to him as if there were one in the air needing to be told. I hadn't known Sam ever to tell this story to anyone but me since I met him—Sam's stories are usually about homey situations, such as the criminal cunning that governs the minds of some people who insist on feeding dogs from the table and so on. He leaves it to me, usually, to tell the adventure stories and is pretty gruff about heroic dog stories most of the time.

"I was stationed on Cam Ranh Bay, where the war dogs were shipped in," Sam was saying. "Spooky, schizy, useless, they were—most of them—by the time they made it there and got released from their crates, but some of them would straighten around. More dogs than men, in fact, would straighten around, and as often as not, with a man-dog patrol unit, the handlers would sleep or doze during duty hours, or sometimes be stoned or drunk. They preferred drunk, but the dogs did their jobs, anyway, staying on patrol sometimes with, in effect, no handler at all, which was maybe, now that I think of it, almost a disadvantage for the Army, since it meant that the sort of guy who would sleep through a patrol survived to sleep through more of them."

Luke said, "It's ironic that it had to matter whether anyone slept through a patrol, when there wasn't anything it was our business to patrol."

Sam said impatiently, "I don't know any more than anyone else what we were doing there, but there we were, and the dogs, even though they didn't know what we were doing there, either, at least they knew what to do once they were there—some of them, anyway. The good ones. Knew how to stay loyal and do their job, which was to guard what they were given to guard. Westmoreland had long since vetoed Galbraith's idea of keeping the troops in enclaves and on the air bases. Westmoreland's idea was that that way the men lose fighting spirit, they can't bear the idea of enclaves. I don't know.

"But dogs don't lose spirit that easily. Dogs were better at being dogs, in Vietnam, than men were at being men, partly because a dog, well, a dog can know about death, but he doesn't keep his mind on it. Vietnam was neither here nor there, but you sure got a chance to see the qualities of a dog worked out in detail. I took dog after dog out of crates, with their courage worn away from shipment, and got to see some of them walk out of their crates after nearly a week in transit, as sane as though the Army knew anything about dogs.

"There was a Vietcong encampment the Army knew about, by inference, but we'd been hunting for months and couldn't turn it up. The Army had been hunting, that is; I was just there on base, training dogs and vetting them.

"A big burly German Shepherd came into the base, walked out of his crate like he was in his own living room, and he took to me, and I took to him too. That was the dog called Zeus. A nose like an angel's dream he had, but he wouldn't use it for anyone but me. Sometimes I try to figure out if I didn't make that happen, wanting the glory of scout patrol, especially with that dog, and every time I ask myself the question, the answer is different, but Zeus and I did end up on scout patrol.

"And Zeus found that encampment."

You could feel his pride in Zeus, but Luke said, "Didn't that mean people got killed?" I thought, *Of course people got killed.* I knew what Sam's story was about now, and I knew why he was telling it to Luke, and I half shivered. He didn't want to lose me as a partner, I figured—I was that dumb then, I didn't see how deep a pledge Sam was making with his story, not just a pledge to a partner—and he was telling Luke to shape up. He'd heard some of the disillusioned-with-questing stuff from Luke, and he had no patience with it. Sam knew about reasons to be disillusioned.

Sam said, "Yes. People got killed. It was a war, just or unjust, and there never was a war people didn't get killed in, even the Cold War, and I'm about to tell you."

Luke said, "Wait a minute. How did you get to Vietnam? Did you volunteer?"

Sam chewed on a drumstick for a moment. Sam had left college for dogs and so was eligible for the draft, but he didn't say that. He may have known what I saw, that Luke's questions came from a kind of naïveté people who are awestruck when they start to find out what dog training really is are subject to— there's a tendency to think that anyone who can do something this wonderful has a kind of control over their world that other people don't, as though dog training were *voluntary*. But Sam just went on, ignoring the question. "The way it is, a handler moves through the jungle, just following the dog, reading the dog's every ear-twitch with more love than he ever reads a woman's smile, and because he's concentrating on the dog, there has to be backup behind him, covering *him*, while the dog covers the jungle. So, on this day, Zeus suddenly moved like a base runner, out through the jungle, out where I had been told there was nothing at all—men, dogs and helicopters had been over it a dozen times. Nothing was there. That was certain.

"But there was nothing to consult unless you count the jungle, and no one to trust except Zeus when he alerted and went forward, and there it was, a valley full of Vietcong, at least several hundred of them.

"Our job was over then. The platoon radioed back, and the air support came and bombed and napalmed the hell out of that valley and the armaments there, while Zeus and I sat up there on the hillside. Having lunch. Hundreds of people getting killed, and all I could think about was what a hell of a dog Zeus was, and it must have gotten to a hundred and twenty-five degrees in the shade, and I thought about that dog working as if it were the first day of spring in Central Park."

Luke puffed his pipe in agitation, got more and more distant and stiff, and said, "Sounds like a good reason why you shouldn't train dogs—all of those people horribly dead because a dog did what you call a good job. Isn't that a reason to stop? Do dog trainers ever respond to reason?" Luke stopped and said, "I don't mean that the way it sounds, Sam. Give me a moment." He rubbed the bowl of his pipe, as he does a lot when he's writing, before relighting it, trying to summon something that got away from him. "I guess I was never in a situation where something like war was a persistent given, three hundred and sixty degrees around me. But didn't you think about how you got there, about what it was meaning?"

"No," said Sam. "I did at first, like my friends, but in war you can get weird, letting the history of a thing get in on top of you, and then you stop thinking at all. There and here, I've had the dogs to think about, and I've learned to think about them." Then he added, "And there are reasons to fret once in a while, but not a reason to stop training, although it might be a good idea to stay out of situations like Vietnam."

Sam's remark might have taken us over, air and all, and I might have been able to tell Luke why there is never a reason to stop training dogs and why reason is to dog training what gardening tools are to a garden—reason isn't *it*. It can help, I wanted to say, but it isn't it. Luke, I saw, was alert to my allegiance to Sam's story, even if he didn't understand that Sam left out the obvious closing, which Sam would never say to Luke, and which goes, "I know all of that and more, and I'm still training dogs, because I'm a dog trainer." Of course, he didn't have a dog of his own, and that was part of the story, and he might have said something about that if Luke . . . or, at that point, I might have, and things might have been different. There are moments when you can say these things.

Sam's story was about what is on the surface, the details you run into, which are everything but which can obsess you, like grief, so that you don't see the light that is in the motion of a dog; when I was at college, wanting to paint it, my teacher said I was talking about truth, and you can call it that—it is something you know in action. You don't sit around knowing it.

However, I didn't say it because at this point Freddie appeared, out of nowhere as usual. He wanted my advice on how to prevent George from leaping up to bite Blue's privates while they were playing leapfrog.

Freddie's red hair waved around his head as he talked. "And I put George on a stand under the utility pole, between the jump standards, but he just curls himself around the pole and goes for Blue, anyway." He added, because there is always something admirable for Freddie about his dogs, "George is real agile, ma'am. The pole is just sitting there on the pins, and George curved up, went for Blue without moving it at all, and Blue just tucked himself up out of the way, in midair, you should see it. I wish I'd had a camera. But I want them to work together better."

Instead of pointing out that there was no practical use for dogs playing leapfrog, because you don't get anywhere that way with Freddie, I suggested having George jump over Blue. I wasn't serious, figuring Freddie wasn't experienced enough to handle the situation, and what I meant was that he should abandon the project, but off he skipped, Blue and George bouncing at heel beside him, to have George do the jumping, over Blue instead of the other way around. Freddie went off happily, actually to take my advice. I started to stop him, but the tension between Sam and Luke made it hard to move.

Sam had Zeus when I met him at a tracking trial. When his tour of duty was over, Sam had been supposed to debrief Zeus so that he could be returned, a Rin-Tin-Tin covered with glory, to his owners, but Zeus had been offered to the Army in the first place because he was a hard dog who offered to bite the family more than once. With Sam, Zeus was every bit as noble and forbearing as any dog you care to name, on or off the screen, but without Sam, even being led around by tough, knowing handlers, he had been iffy.

Anyway, Sam hadn't worked very hard at debriefing him, he told me, and went through the red tape until he got to go home with the dog. He didn't talk much about how he went through the red tape, but since it was Sam, I imagine that he just walked through quietly so that you couldn't tell from the outside there could be a problem. Zeus was—well, when I thought of the perfect White German Shepherd, I thought of something like Zeus, only white. He had humor too.

I met Sam and Zeus at a tracking trial, where I had Duke. Zeus could track any way you please. First nose to the ground, footprint to footprint, then sliding along with his nose four inches above the ground if the wind and air were good for that, and when he changed from one scenting posture to another, it was so fast that it was like two frames in a film with some intervening footage cut out. One instant he was frozen *this* way; the next, he was *that* way and moving.

In the house he would "practice" these moves, only now from one frozen frame to the next, while "tracking" something imaginary, and it would stop conversation all right, but Zeus was serious enough to bite off the hot end of the galaxy, too, and he would have if he hadn't had respect for creation.

Zeus died in midair, at around thirteen years old, going over an obstacle course. Sam kept saying he didn't get it. "Dammit, if a dog is well enough to go through the course, he *can't* die, there isn't a way for such a dog to die at such a moment," as if decline, pain and kidney failure would have been better, and as if Sam didn't get it—of course he got it, that's what people mean when they say they don't get it.

I thought back to Zeus, with Sam and Luke talking quietly and fairly politely about something else until Freddie returned a bit later to say that my suggestion had worked out so well that now he could even get George to stand right, without biting, while Blue jumped.

Sam retired to his cottage after clearing up, talking with Luke being such heavy water then, so it was just me and Luke and some lemonade and Homer. Luke talked some about Sam's story, asking why Sam had told it and then saying that he hoped Sam had outgrown that sort of thing. I didn't know what "that sort of thing was," and didn't then know a lot of things, but Freddie's dogs were performing, and it didn't seem like a time to worry about it. It wasn't sensible for Freddie to have succeeded, but Freddie was at his best when he wasn't sensible. There was no reason my non-advice should have worked, and it wouldn't have if either Freddie or George had been sensible.

Freddie grinned at his triumph and said, "Miss Diane, you were absolutely right. After George jumped over Blue, he stood still for Blue to jump over him. I guess he just wanted some symmetry. They did it like this and this," he said, his hands jumping over each other. I started to explain that I hadn't been any help, but how could I prove anything in front of the reality of the dogs? Sometimes the truth just happens to you.

We were applauding George and Blue, because, of course, Freddie showed us what the dogs could do while he talked about it. Even Homer barked approval. Homer is not one to go in for high jinks, but he is generous and polite and thereby can care about the other dogs and their new shows; he didn't forget Freddie, either—went over to lick his hand when the show was done.

Four
LUKE
STARTS
A STORY

Luke had an even longer story, one night soon after Sam's story about Zeus.

Maybe Luke wouldn't have told his story if I hadn't mentioned Zeus—Luke had asked me again what temperament was. He meant, what did I want in the White German Shepherd, and I said that there was no way to get what I wanted from a White German Shepherd, but that if there were, it would be something like what Zeus gave Sam, a dog willing something, willing one thing with clarity no matter what.

When Luke drove down to the kennel that afternoon—I had been working Homer on a longish track—it took him about forty-five minutes to work it through.

The Irish Wolfhound standard has for some time started with the phrase, "Of great size and commanding appearance." People write books and books trying to improve on that opening.

Homer is even bigger—and a lot sounder—than most Wolfhounds, which are the tallest breed of all. Homer weighs one hundred and seventy-seven pounds and stands thirty-eight and a half inches at the withers, which means that when I'm standing up, I don't have to put my hand lower than my ribs to pat him. He can lick my chin with all four feet on the ground, and when all four feet aren't on the ground, as when he jumps up to put his paws on my shoulders and stand up, I look straight forward at about the middle of his chest.

Homer is a tracker. One time he tracked a kid who had wandered off through a gigantic parking lot, a blacktop surface, on a hot day—103°—and the part of the track on the blacktop took over an hour, but he didn't quit till he found the place where the track led out into the park.

This evening I had been working a practice track. Homer hadn't had any serious tracks to do for a while, so I worked him on one every so often so he wouldn't lose the interest and the feel. This one I had Sam lay for me. It had fresh hamburger beside it, to see if he could be distracted, then it went through rough stubble and over a stone wall, and even though there's no question by now about whether Homer will keep on a track, there might be an eventual question of his getting tired, old, maybe even lame, and also, if you're me, you never get to take that kind of dog work for granted.

Freddie helped with the distractions by having George cross the track with him, and even got George to jump Homer once when he paused to work out a problem (Homer never became a particularly flashy tracker, just dead on target every time, and I must say that having a Samoyed jump him was a new one, even for Homer, but on he went, and my heart gave a light, sharp jump.)

There was nothing in the world for me but Homer's work, but just as we were finishing, Luke appeared, and instead of thinking over what had happened with Homer, I thought about hugging Luke. There wasn't an inch of me that wasn't aware of every splendid inch of Luke and how to fit into it, into the ease and grace of the shape and movement of him.

Then I thought about being too hot and dirty and smelly to be hugging him, especially since his shirt and pants were spotless. I realized this while I was halfway through the hug, and that was some of the trouble. That was the sort of reason I used to keep my love life out of the kennel, that sort of interruption of training thought. Not that Luke had ever said anything about dirt, but he kept wearing cream-colored slacks, and this was the evening he told much more of his story.

I went inside and washed up, changed from my shirt into a blouse you couldn't work dogs in, and Homer, with his long, hard bones, lay on the hook rug, covering it. Once in a while he would lift his head to attend gravely to some sound or scent, and whenever he did, I'd watch him until he relaxed again with that funny, frustrated sense-of-responsibility kind of sigh dogs have, but the rest of the time I was just being there on the couch with Luke, who had put a John Coltrane album on, the one called *A Love Supreme*, where you can listen and almost get to wanting nothing more than the swoop and glide of that horn. Luke was smoking his pipe, the smoke going up and around like the horn, easy, exact and meditative, like the essence of Luke himself.

Luke sometimes has an odd way of putting things, odd and perfect. "Homer keeps you informed of the night," he said this time.

"Well, it's his job to keep watch."

"That's what I mean. That's nice. Scary but nice."

I took notice of this, especially since I didn't really get what he meant when he talked about Sam's Vietnam story. "Homer won't hurt you, so how is it scary?"

"It's partly you. You walk out there, walking into some knowledge, I think, and I don't know what the dogs tell you about. It's different from the ranch, for me at least. That was a lot bigger than your kennel, but the ranch was all a kind of living room, a kind of order. It had a daytime order to it, except during storms, even at night. I learned to love that from Esther—she valued safety and warmth for herself and everyone. You're not after that, you're after all of these visions—white dogs, movies."

Crankiness took hold of me like a fever, and I could have pointed out that Homer brought kids home safe, but what I said was, "What else is there to be after?" But I didn't feel cranky in time to avoid noticing that actually I was pretty poor, and perhaps Luke was noticing this.

Then I remembered that I spent a lot of money on dog equipment and books that Luke probably spent making his life decent. The only thing I had that anyone else but a dog trainer might want was my Toyota, but it was getting on now. The house was small, the furniture ragbag and the car old, just because I didn't ever have the money at the right moment and not because I was so poor. I was just about to think that the noble thing to do was probably to be like Esther, with a big, nice ranch house and miles of well-kept fence and dark honey hair, when Luke went on to say something sarcastic about Zeus and noble dogs and people getting killed.

Then I got angry with Luke and pointed out firmly to myself that I had washed up after working Homer, used scent, tucked in my clean blouse and if there were one or two twigs in my hair, what did a person want, anyway?

This reminded me that I was about the only woman I'd ever known who had twigs in her hair after she washed up, which meant other women had discipline that I lacked, which is why their hair went smooth for them, and this was another thing that I didn't believe, I just thought it.

So that's how I was the night Luke told me the story of his life, or one of the nights. People have to keep telling the story of their lives, of course, trying to get it right, and probably Luke wouldn't have said much that night about his life if he had known how many mats had gotten into my thinking, like in an ungroomed Afghan's coat. Luke was trying to get the mats out of his thinking by telling me; he said he hadn't had to rethink who he was until I started looking for the White German Shepherd, until he heard Sam's story about Zeus.

What he told me about was being young, in 1969, and thinking about wanting to write. He had graduated but held on to his student apartment in Berkeley, resisting the temptation to take a job that paid something. He was on the staff of the *San Francisco Chronicle* for a while, but it seemed to him that free-lance work was the thing he had to do, to learn real writing, the writing that would awaken America, so he saved a bit of money and left the *Chronicle*.

He talked about how he couldn't find a woman who would have him for long, and how he used to think it was just as well, maybe, because there was the writing.

He talked about writing as a kind of quest, and he talked about how all quests, all efforts for anything beyond ordinary happiness, were dangerous, and more dangerous to people around the quester, like the people around Ahab in *Moby Dick*.

There was a pause, during which I went insane for a moment and wondered if he wasn't right about quests, and maybe looking for a White German Shepherd was like looking for the aurora borealis—what if you found it?

Then Luke put his hand on my breast, and I forgot everything except his touch and the way it spread from my loins by way of the marrow in my bones, and I felt this to be dangerous, which is why I pushed away from Luke a bit, saying, "We can't now, Jerry Slough is bringing a dog by for me to look at."

Luke straightened up, saying, "Okay, okay," and started to tell me more of his story. In college there were things he read that stayed with him. Milton's *Aereopagetica:* "Self-reliance"; "Civil Disobedience."

Yeats came along for him, in that inexplicable way poets will, the later Yeats reflecting on the work of the earlier one, work that had given imaginative substance to an insurrection, and he quoted to me from a poem called "Man and Echo," where it asks, "Did that play of mine send out/Certain men the English shot?"

I said that was more futility than I wanted in my living room just now, and I thought to myself that in a day or two he could work Homer. If Homer retrieved for him, maybe it would wash out the later Yeats. I don't know if you understand—futility was just Luke's disguise—and I decided that I would insist that he work right so that Homer would retrieve for him, looking and breathing and thinking the way clouds would if ice crystals could darken and run smooth at hound speed.

Five
A DIRTY
DOG

I t got late, and there was Luke going on with his story. I couldn't tell whether he was confessing or bragging; neither, probably, or both, because he didn't know. Bragging, I thought, was the appropriate response—Luke was a *writer*. He had formed the idea of a journalism so powerful that people reading it would find it, for a while at least, impossible to tolerate injustice and oppression, much less engage in it, a journalism that had the power of fiction. When the right stories happened, Luke would tell them; and he never ran out of material. The mere actualities of Vietnam, say, the bits on TV, were too sprawled, too inchoate, to give anyone a frame for thinking, acting. And the energy was there, the audience was there; girls were giving flowers to policemen, for christsake.

I kept waiting for Luke to sound stupid, saying all of this, but it sounded all right to me, who never had been part of the dreams of the sixties.

Still, by now, of course, I knew what was coming and didn't know if I wanted it to come, so I got up to pour more wine while I waited for it to come, loving him and thinking of reminding him that there's a difference between imagining heroic action and doing it, and reminding him that Martin Luther King, Jr., had, somewhere in all of this, emerged able to tell people that freedom meant being free of the fear of death. He could do that, but could we? And so what if we couldn't? But Luke knew all of that and still told his story. He had to, and not only because of Sam's story.

Luke with his typewriter, Sam with Zeus, had found out that power really is power. But Sam had steadied back into training, though he didn't have a dog of his own; Luke had changed the center of his world. I thought of saying, "Look, for King, urging risks on people was a way of helping them to wake up, and to be awake was what mattered," and then I was going to say, almost did as I handed him his wine, "Okay, mind your silly manners if you like, be as cautious as hell, but don't give that stuff to me." Maybe if I had said that, Luke might have taken off right then.

But I didn't say it. Luke said, "After that, after the girls and the flowers and whatever it was on a given day, I went and drank with some of the cops I knew when they came off duty. One night one cop said he hated it, it was confusing and in a weird way boring—I'm not sure the cop actually said, 'weird,' but he said it was like some kind of fear tired him out worse than any kind of active work, and he had always thought his weapons were for thugs, anyway, not students, and he said he could hear his own father's voice when he thought that way, telling him it wasn't a man's way of thinking.

"I could hear my father's voice, for that matter, worrying that I was embroiled with this kind of journalism; both of my parents tended to be anxious about me."

The sudden appearance of Luke's parents in this was nerve-racking, so I said, after several such more tales, including one about the horribly racist ways some cops talked, saying things like "nigger," and "ornamental" instead of "Oriental."

"Most of the time a cop is just a cop, you know." I don't know why I said that—it didn't seem to be true, but I added, "Luke, dammit, have you ever actually been on the beat with a uniformed cop? They have to make the distinction between niggers and blacks, you know. I don't know how often a cop gets it right, but niggers are the ones who will kill you and me, and the cop too. It's a cop's distinction, not a civilian's."

Luke said that he wished cops were a little more careful about their distinctions, then, and I wondered how in hell he had managed to be a journalist as he told me another Luke-ish story about this one cop. He had had a turn at it, the young girl handing him a flower, or trying to, and when he wouldn't accept it, the girl sticking the stem into the pin that held his badge on, and this cop had, of course, remained stiff, on duty, but one night with Luke, when the whiskey had reached the right level, he said, "Looking at that girl, my stomach wept. My goddamn bones wept. Do you think I'm crazy?"

Then Luke had written his stories about cops, even the secret weeping in the bodies of policemen, on the basis of which he urged more marches, more flowers, and *Ramparts* had bought the story. Luke was dizzy with the power of being fully alive—he was making a bit of money, but mostly he was inexhaustible, trying for a complete vision of a new America. I saw these stories, and they aren't quaint, you think they'd sound a little dusty now, but Luke wasn't like some in the sixties, feeling important and committed, getting on the bandwagon. He was writing, writing the way Sam and I trained.

He was on hand at Kent State, and of course he invited his readers to doubt that all policemen had tears of that sort in them; simpler explanations, traditional ones, were usually accurate enough for day-to-day purposes. He doubted that the governor of California wept. Money and power were *opposable* forces.

His genius was for the tiny stories, like the one about the policeman, so while he reported the huge stories, he reported as though the largest events turned on the fulcrum of a single human gesture. He had dreams, ordinary ones, one in which a girl flung a flower at a National Guardsman, and as it touched him, his weapons powdered and blew away in the breeze, lace mantles in the air, like dogwood.

"Lace mantles?" I said, not knowing what dogwood looked like, but it was the writing he wanted to talk about, so he replied to my interruption by offering to pour some more wine. I didn't answer, and he didn't move to pour it but went on.

It didn't seem to matter what he wrote. He wrote telling people that they had power—farm workers, students, blacks, Indians, housewives, even bankers. The power to tell people this was his power.

When Isla Vista broke, he went there, expenses paid by *Ramparts*. Isla Vista began as a protest, largely against the Bank of America as slum landlord, and became a hell, a riot that, viewed on TV in California, settled the issue about student protesters in a lot of people's minds overnight. People started working it out that, as it was the cops with the weapons and the students who were getting hurt . . . anyway, this one became a riot with the possibly unwitting help of Ronald Reagan, governor of California then, who liked to see that the National Guard and other police forces had plenty of experience. And Isla Vista smoked, in fact and in the mind.

However, Luke didn't cover Isla Vista, not in the way he had intended. He arrived in a bold mood and roved and dodged through the scene, listening, watching, registering faces, hesitations, gestures, forward surgings. He came on many scenes: a policeman handcuffing a tall, skinny boy who barely had a beard and who had, he noted, strangely mild eyes; a girl, in jeans and a tight halter top that revealed the nipples of achingly young breasts, was clinging to the boy, trying to pull him away from the policeman. And a second policeman swung his nightstick against her bare back, savagely, and as the girl lost her hold on the boy and stumbled back, he swung again, at her head, and dodging, she fell. The first policeman raised his stick, and Luke, without thought, fell forward between the cop and the girl, covering her with his body, feeling the shock of pain in his shoulders as he hit the ground with his arms stiffened to keep his weight off her.

Caught up in his tale, I said that that was something I wouldn't have had the courage to do.

"It wasn't courage. I just did it. I might have done it at Kent State, but I didn't. I might have done it at any moment, seeing cops harass people in the city, but I didn't. It wasn't thought or courage."

"If it wasn't courage, then what is courage?"

"No, it was just that fragile cotton top she had on, her bare back exposed to the club, and her breasts, and anyway, I was pretty certain I wouldn't get hurt. I figured that cop was just alert enough to read me correctly as the press and knew his chief wouldn't want him at the center of a story about clubbing coeds. I didn't think this consciously at the time. All I knew at the time was her halter top, her youth."

Luke asked the cop for an ambulance for the girl. It was half an hour before it arrived, and during that time Luke stayed crouched over her. She seemed unconscious at first, then moved and groaned. Luke hushed her somehow, though she was heading for panic. He asked about the pain, was relieved to see her legs move. Once someone, running, tripped over him, nearly knocking him away from her. She asked, "What happened?" He replied, "You've been hurt. It's going to be okay. Lie still. An ambulance is coming."

She crumpled again and closed her eyes, curled on her side, revealing the reddening and more on her back, where the nightstick had landed. She asked, over and over, "What happened?" He replied, over and over again, "Lie still. You've been hurt. An ambulance is coming."

Luke said that while the riot swirled around them, his crouching over the girl had become the only human, definable action in what was now a world of madness and smoke. Even when the major activity moved away from their area, he remained over her, not noticing the effort of it until he went to get up and felt what the strain had done to his joints and muscles. He thought later that in that half hour something had left him, but he couldn't name it and wasn't sure it had been his in the first place.

In the hospital he got from her the name of the aunt who had raised her; she was an orphan. He called the aunt, who lived half an hour away in a ranch on the hills, north and inland. She came, talked to the girl, whose name was Carrie, was worried but not hysterical.

"When Carrie fell asleep, it was after two in the morning, so I offered to find Esther, her aunt, a motel, and she accepted, and she was glad of the company. We had a sandwich out of the machine in the hospital, and I took her to her motel, planning to go back to the riot, but somehow I stayed with her. We didn't screw, and we didn't say much, either.

"Esther only trembled once, saying, 'What's happened to the world?' I had no idea, then, what she meant by 'the world.' That was the only time I ever saw Esther tremble, and it wasn't to protect her that I stayed.

"I quit journalism that night, and there's no particular explanation at all. History accidentally caught me watching over the sleep of a woman, that's all."

History, and one or two other things, had left me watching over the sleep of a few people, including Sam, and I have watched over a child's sleep and a dog's, and mine has been watched over, and it didn't cause me to turn, never did. I had not before loved anyone who had been caused to turn, to turn away. Maybe I would have but for this or that, but I didn't, and I didn't know what turning away meant, though I knew Sam had been in danger of it and hadn't, because he knew he would have lost his knowledge if he had turned to stay still. Dogs move, and we move with them, turn toward them as they turn, and that's the only way we know anything. But maybe, I thought, Luke meant something else, though I didn't think so.

This was also the first time I had loved someone besides Sam, who had something to turn from. No matter what Luke said or did, you could see the reality of him.

I couldn't ask Luke because his story lost what continuity it had had. He kept telling them that a boy was killed, that there had been a boy killed by the cops, shot while trying to talk the rioters into stopping. Carrie, it turned out, had crippling bruises, but the X rays said her back would be okay. Luke and Esther stayed two more days while Carrie was in the hospital, and Luke returned the Hertz car *Ramparts* was paying for and drove in Esther's car, Esther in the passenger seat and Carrie resting in the back, up to Esther's ranch.

The ranch was a wonder to Luke, milk cows as well as steer, a ranch manager, small cottages and house trailers inhabited by some of the cowboys, one cowboy whose semi-independent business was making cheese from some of the milk, the gruffness of the cowboys, sometimes the cliché violence of them, mostly in roaring talk. Luke had only heard of such things, or seen them from a reporter's distance.

Then he learned that Carrie had been at Isla Vista in the first place because of an article of Luke's, the one in *The New Republic* about history turning on the fulcrum of a single human gesture.

"So I stopped. I turned the story into *Ramparts*. It was about the dangers of journalism in such situations. They paid me for it but didn't print it."

My throat muscles started to do something, but that wasn't the moment, because Homer sat up and put his gaze directly before me, and my throat softened again as he lay back down, with his ribs just touching my leg. I wanted to tell Sam's story again, as if I could change Luke's autobiography that way, and maybe I could have, or maybe I could have told about not throwing your heart in the grave after the dog, because it sounded like it wasn't just journalism that Luke had quit, but journalism-for-instance, and dogs were another instance of it, and so was I. *Don't leave me, Luke.*

"And I married Esther. No more writing, because no matter what I wrote, it would do harm, incalculable harm. When I even thought of the typewriter, I thought of the cop's club, the boy falling." I thought, Dogs are only carnivores, but humans are omnivores, and still didn't see why Luke didn't say that death is the only alternative to eating and moving. And the good, insofar as it is in us, eats and moves, and movement is sacred, and I could have said it but felt shy. *Movement is sacred.* That's what Sam had said. Homer looked uneasily at Luke, hearing something in his tone, but we kept quiet. I didn't want Luke to move his hand from my breast, where I could trace the eloquent shape of him with my hand.

He talked in uncertain scraps about life on the ranch, the idea of order, the one space cleared for human contact.

Esther had a rosewood table she loved, polished, kept fresh flowers and ferns on, so I asked what Esther looked like. Blond, tallish, kept her hair turned at the nape of her neck, and I saw the back of that neck bent slightly to adjust a few leaves of fern while Luke said that one chose one thing or another, a quest or the imperfections of a possible order, a clearing, herding cattle, meals, sleep, loyalty to a few persons, because that was the only loyalty possible.

I hadn't heard anyone use the word *quest* before now, and it wasn't Luke, but me, who turned—jerked away, really—suddenly conscious of the cheap, homemade pine table in front of us with its jumble of training tackle, including the harness

Homer had worn that day, which was getting past repair in places and was not clean. I touched my head for comfort and found a bit of leaf there and pulled it out.

Homer lifted his head as Prince came trotting out from the bedroom where he had been sleeping for a while, but I didn't look at them, and I couldn't refuse to acknowledge to myself what Luke had to say about his life with Esther: I wanted to, but there was no logic for it except the logic of life whose axioms are beyond the dimensions of safety. For example, next time I make love with Luke, his heart or mine may stop, and how could I say that in less than twenty years? Loyalty to a few persons, I thought—yes, but loyalty to an idea as well.

What I did was to unbuckle Homer's harness and take out the stitching that held the buckle in place, preparing it for restitching, and God knows what Luke was thinking.

Luke drained his wine and headed for the kitchen and came back with more wine and a rag to wipe the coffee rings from the table, but he didn't complete the effort because I stopped him—he was about to tangle the harness.

As Luke waved the rag, trying for a moment to clean the table without disturbing the harness, Prince decided to clown, barking at the rag and growling as though his ancestors were terriers. Then Luke put the rag back and came and sat next to me again, saying, "It wasn't just Esther and the ranch. Esther is dead, and I've left the ranch and I'll never write that way again. But you want to *train* that way, and there will be the movie."

I said, "Well, this movie isn't going to cause any riots. It's just a kid's movie, so even if there were any more student riots, this movie wouldn't fuel them, and there aren't any more protests like those." It was hard to sound cross. Against my will, the love I felt for him blanketed and silenced the room.

And then I was about to try to defend my coffee table when Homer moved suddenly toward the window and then the door, his full height caught in the curve of his neck. Prince stayed by him, barking once or twice and trying to look as tall as Homer, and then there was the sound of a car in the gravel driveway; headlights shone on the window, and all of the dogs barked. I thought of some half-funny stories I had heard from a friend from Kentucky, about how the wealthy can afford to have one dog, the working classes two or three, but the bums are so poor, they have a dozen each. I was a bum of sorts. The kennel was no cattle ranch landscaped with oak trees, and I didn't even know how to go about buying furniture polish.

I pulled open the door to find Jerry Slough standing there with a dog of sorts. It was a White German Shepherd, or might be once it was cleaned up. Right now it was covered with dirt and feces, I figured, by the smell; obviously Slough had been tying the dog up short for days, or engaging in some other of his versions of kennel management. Jerry is what gets called a fly-by-night guard-dog trainer, but his legal troubles weren't caused by greed or dishonesty. He just wasn't old enough yet, didn't know enough, wasn't strong enough in character. He's not vicious—in his own way he's a real visionary. But we're all true visionaries in this business. Sam hates Jerry, whereas I merely can't stand him, which is why I'm always the one Jerry comes to when he has a dog for us to look at. Jerry sometimes gets courage and viciousness confused, like a lot of people. Goes to the pound, takes the meanest dog he can find, "trains" it for an hour or two, and sells it as a sentry dog for a few hundred dollars, sometimes more, sometimes less, depending.

Despite himself, he has an eye for a dog. That's his pride and my interest; sometimes he ends up with a nice dog—quite often, really—and fortunately he's too lazy and confused to do much with the dog so that if people don't end up with a trained dog, at least they have a decent one often enough and, often enough, not something really dangerous.

When Jerry miscalculates a dog's background, I find the dog in my class and on the other end of a leash I have to handle for a while, for rehabilitation, or else Sam has to do it. Sam blames Jerry for the dogs more than I do, I guess.

Just then, Jerry wasn't something I felt like introducing to Luke, not at that particular moment, with the room full of the scent of polished rosewood tables. Jerry's small, with a greenish-brown complexion. He moves in and out of town, packing up whenever some client gets irate enough to call a lawyer. But Jerry—this is either the worst part or the best—Jerry actually believes in what he is doing, has an idea in his head of the transcendentally vicious dog, or the transcendentally protective one. That's what he's looking for, a dog who would love only Jerry.

And there was Jerry with another goddamn trashy White German Shepherd—underfed, to boot. With such situations it can be a month or more before you find out what you've got or even if you have anything. Or that's what I saw then, with Luke behind me, my mind full of a vision of cut flowers and crystal.

I told Jerry, "Sorry, that's not it, that's not what we're looking for."

"Hey-ya, Di, where d'you think you're going to do better? His name's Jouster." Jerry reached the leash toward me, and Homer, behind me, advanced so that his head commanded the doorway.

"Jerry, thank you, but that's really not the right dog."

The dog he had with him was reaching his head forward, to sniff noses with Homer, so I added that I didn't want a dogfight. Homer never fights other dogs unless they're hurting someone or they jump him, but Jerry backed off with the filthy dog, shaking his head at me for all the world, like a punk threatening someone with loss of manhood for not buying his dope or his stolen TV or something, but feebly, in imitation.

With Luke beside me, I watched Jerry load the dog into his van before I closed the door on him and went back in.

Luke said, "That looked to me like a good-sized Shepherd."

"Mmm."

"Wasn't the pigmentation right? I mean, the black eyes and nose were there—what you told me you wanted."

"Luke! Who's running this kennel?"

"I'm sorry. I just wanted to understand what you saw wrong with the dog, because he looked good to me."

"The dog was all right. He just wasn't . . ." I pictured the dog, making my memory go into slow motion so I could examine it, and then the rosewood and the cut flowers vanished and it hit me. If that dog washed up all right, chances were very, very, very good that that was the dog I was looking for. I realized it when I remembered the way he'd arched his back and tucked in his rear end, jumping, back into the van. An eye as clear and dark and bold as you could want, and that hind end! Taut, springy, smoother than the best daydreams of the people who design shocks for Porsche, and sure of himself.

I remembered him not backing down when he confronted Homer—and not pushing, either. There's courtesy for you, not a hair raised, or at least none of the hairs that were free enough of filth so you could tell, and hell, if he washed up clean, with no biscuit, that was the dog.

I didn't have to remember this. I'd seen the dog as one with presence right away. All my senses were on green alert, but the message didn't reach my intelligence, which was otherwise distractedly stumbling around, until Slough's truck had left the driveway.

I couldn't see a dog in front of my nose, and there is no explanation for this except that I am not a dog trainer. Dog training is an either/or thing. There I was with Luke. There was the dog, or rather, there the dog was not. Maybe I didn't see him for some rag end of psychology. I don't know, it doesn't matter. Something cruel some boy said to me, or that I thought some boy said to me when I was thirteen? I can't remember much about being thirteen, so if that was it at some point, it isn't anymore. If I'd been with Sam, I would have seen him.

Luke said later in the night that Esther's love was the only thing that had made him feel that writing a good novel wasn't essential to him as a reason for being alive. This ticked me off a bit, so I said, "Well, you've got to do *something*. Write a bad novel!" Luke said he wouldn't, and left for a few minutes, coming back with more wine and a typing-paper box. It was full of around a dozen beginnings of novels. Some were no more than two or three pages; one or two were around fifty pages long.

All of them were striking enough to make me forget to worry, except for one story that was one of those intellectual male-guilt trips. I said, "But this stuff is good!" And thought, *No guilt in my kennel.* And thought, *What do you know about it, Diane Brannigan?*

"And unfinished," said Luke. "I still want to finish one, Di." He straightened the paper and took the box away and came back, and I forgot what I had meant to say to him about my pine table with its tack and coffee rings, or even that I thought there was something to say, and we dropped the subject.

Pretty soon we went to bed, where rosewood tables came back briefly, memories of the dog Slough had brought more strongly. I didn't know what rosewood looked like, anyway, but dogs I did know, and I faked an orgasm, which Luke didn't seem to notice me doing. Then I lay there with him for a while, telling myself not to worry; how was Jerry going to sell the dog between tonight and tomorrow morning? I would call in the morning and take another look—without Luke around, since he had to go out on a couple of interviews for the *Herald.* I could go pick up the dog without worrying about defending myself doing business with such a person as Jerry Slough. About whom Luke, of course, had said nothing.

Six
IN WHICH
NO ONE
ACTS BUT
JOUSTER

In the morning I awoke thinking about the fact that the dog was there, in Jurupa, and that mattered more than any waverings on any dog trainer's part. The dog was what mattered, and the dog had shown up. I waited until ten o'clock to call Slough, who is a night owl when he can be. While I was waiting, I kissed Luke a lot, and he responded as though he'd never studied anything but happiness, and if I hadn't had the phone call to make, we would have spent the morning learning more and more about the radiance of skin. It didn't matter so much that I'd goofed about the dog that morning, I felt more than reprieved: We would get the dog. There had been a cool rain, the dust of Jurupa was washed out of the air, off the horizon. It was like that—the air we all breathed forgave and was forgiven because the dog had found us.

When I called, Jerry was just on his way out to deliver the dog to someone named Skeffington, who had a business— Skeffington Auto Parts—for which he wanted protection. His wrecking yard was a very tiny step up the valley from Slough— socially, that is—but Skeffington at least had sense enough to buy the dog straight off, and I didn't.

Just for self-torment, I went by the yard later, and after a bath, that dog was so white, he'd show up against new snow and make it fade without any fancy camera tricks. He glittered as if his coat weren't really white at all but clear, like crystal, only so thick that it added up to white.

I passed the yard once, and then went back and stopped off. I bought a radiator hose for the Toyota, and a radio. Picking the radio took a while, and I got a good one, and while I was doing it, I got to watch the dog at work, finding his own work, and he was good, much better than Skeffington seemed to realize, because he said the dog hadn't barked at anyone— Skeffington wanted him to be mean, I guess. The dog watched everything and everyone and made more sense of the place than the Skeffingtons could. I worked out how much money I had, and how much Kaye or the studio might be good for, and made a sizable offer when Skeffington started complaining that he didn't think the dog would hurt anyone. He was interested, but Mrs. Skeffington was so pleased with the way the dog's coat showed off her bracelets when she petted him that she wouldn't hear of selling. Honest, that's what she said. I guess the bracelets were expensive—I can't tell.

On the way home I thought about how I would tell Sam I had tried to buy the dog, and how I would add that maybe that dog wouldn't last long as a jewelry display case. Sam would just say we'd lost the dog and should forget it.

Sam would have reason on his side as usual, so I didn't talk to Luke about it, although he asked. I said he wouldn't know, anyway, he wouldn't know, and he said he hadn't been the one to turn the dog away, and I said that was true, but that he wouldn't know, so he went outside to work Prince on scent, he *said,* but mostly he hung around within view of the window in the kitchen, where I was doing accounts. He looked like someone who was ready to make up, but I was too miserable to care and decided that the next day would be plenty of time to make up, if such things were still possible for a dog trainer who had lost a dog while distracted.

■

It was still sinking in that I had really lost the dog when I went out to where Sam and Freddie were finishing the evening pickup and hosing the runs to tell Sam about it. First I had to tell him that the dog had been around the night before, of course, and I did that part easily enough while I watched Blue, studying one or two trees, and Freddie stopping to watch Blue and to dream of long nights following his dog through the cunning woods. You have to climb mountains to find woods in them in this part of the world, and I have no idea if the woods have coons or not, I'd never seen any, but that didn't stop Freddie from dreaming. The first time I talked to Freddie about anything but his work in class with Blue he had asked, "Ma'am, where do I find raccoons?" He had had with him *The Complete Coon Hunter's Handbook.* I said I had no idea, and he nodded and said thank you, and didn't hold it against me. When we got to know each other a little better, he showed me how he had taught Blue to stand up against a tree and bark, and he said, of course, he didn't really look like he'd treed a coon, but it did show off how well he was built to do that.

George cavorted meanwhile, his Samoyed-white coat shaking off sunshine as he happily assaulted the water from the pressure hose.

Cleaning the runs had pretty much vanished as a problem for us; Freddie, doing it alone, did a better job than Sam and I working together, and in less time, too, because Sam and I kept stopping to talk when we did it, and all the while Freddie worked, he was teaching his dogs things; George would retrieve the end of the pressure hose when it dropped and went snaking around, for example. Freddie had said he got the idea from George's attacks on the hose.

But I'm delaying now for the same reason I delayed that morning. As long as it was just me who knew about losing the dog—Luke couldn't really *know,* he could only sympathize and believe me—it might not be so, but when Sam and I both know the same thing about a dog, then it's true.

Sam and I were walking together looking over the runs, even though by now we knew that Freddie's work was as reliable as his dogs were, and it should have been easy just to say that Slough had already sold the dog. But I also had to tell him the truth about how I had missed getting the dog, because it was Sam as much as me, and we told each other things, though I'd never had such a thing as this to tell him. So I hesitated and yammered and said, "Sam, I . . ." three times, like a schoolgirl trying to confess to something, and Sam, who hadn't had a good night by the looks of him, and was uneasy about having an amateur living at the kennel, anyway, was already angry before I got the important part out, and made no use at all of the sweet wisdom of friendship.

"So you turned away the dog because you were—what? Too busy checking out the goddamn crease of your outfit, worried about your fancy-pants lover?"

I figured he had been with Jenny, whom he sees once every month or so, and used to see, for a year or two, every day and night. Every time Sam and Jenny see each other, no matter whose star is ascending, they come away from each other tense, incomplete. Jenny is thin, full of movement and of books, plays, music. I'd call her *geared* if she were a dog. Sam isn't her only lover; her other one sells computers in Hong Kong, I think.

Jenny's wiriness is resilient stuff, but even so, she seems almost to flutter around Sam's stolid, gallant, slow-moving ways, a Poodle to his Bouvier, and they eat each other up, and Sam let it show that morning. He knows that I know, but I won't say anything; we leave our love lives mostly alone. Usually we left our love lives alone, but the air was getting crowded now.

I thought maybe by the next day the dog would have snapped at someone and the Skeffingtons would sell the dog back to us, so I called, this time offering almost as much as the dog was worth, untrained. We didn't have the amount of money he was worth, but I was still counting on Kaye. It was no good.

The Skeffingtons hadn't any idea what he was worth, but they were still delighted with the way he looked, in the front office, when the customers came in.

After that call I went outside to the runs and picked up and hosed, even though Freddie had done it earlier, and squeegeed them dry and then stood and stared at the reflections in a small pool of water formed where the cement was uneven, and I did not feel sensible.

I am Diane, Ms. Brannigan, Di, and sometimes, and only to Sam, Annie. Sometimes, once in a while, Sam is Abe to me, as on an occasion or two when the perplexities and the grief over Zeus became a uselessness of rage for him. Or as on this occasion, when Sam, wanting to make contact after his flare of temper over Luke and the White German Shepherd, said, "I like this little bitch, Annie, don't you?" next to me in the run there.

I said I did, and relaxed as the world tilted back to normal. She was a little tricolored English Cocker, satiny and warm. She jumped on me when Sam spoke, and I automatically brought my knee up into her chest, the usual correction, and she sat, puzzled and startled but not whining, not a coward. Good.

I told Sam I had tried to buy the dog again, and he just said, "Yeah," too, and we talked about what kind of worker the little English Cocker would make. Sam bent to stroke her, feeling the clean bones as exactly carved as anything Michelangelo ever cared about.

"She's going to work hot," Sam said, straightening up to stand squarely balanced, as he always does. "She'd do just about anything for me I wanted her to do. And she's got a chance."

"Yes." She had a chance, because her owner was too busy rather than too stupid to do all the work on his dogs, and this one would get a chance to use her quick, birdy brain in the field.

Sam said, "Burt's Teamsters Union." I waited. Burt was her owner. "But I think he's a fairly honest crook. Honest with his dogs, anyhow." Then he started telling me about an incident in his class the night before. Just as he started, Luke came up, and I wished that Luke knew what Sam knew about what you have to do and be to be honest with a hard, thorough-working dog. There was nothing wrong with Luke, but he didn't know that. Prince was a good dog, and Luke had done fine with him, but the glory of a Sheltie is how polite he is; a Sheltie will adjust himself when you do it sloppily, doesn't test you as much as some other dogs do. Luke was lucky to have a Sheltie when he did, but it meant he didn't know why training and the kennel had to take everything Sam and I had. He knew he felt better when he started training Prince, but he didn't know how much falseness and confusion presses on people and shows up in training failures, how much it took to clear that away. The movie, if it turned out right, would be a picture of the clearing; when a dog and a handler get it together, there's room in the field for truth.

What truth? Luke would want to know. The truth of that movement.

The night before, there had been a pretty bad dude in class, with a Dobie who was pretty nice but who had been phony-baloneyed into thinking it was cute to attack other dogs. You get this with macho bad dudes and with pillars of the community mostly; morality confuses things no matter what form it takes. Sam had grabbed the dog's leash as he was lunging for the

Bearded Collie next to him, and the dude had pulled a knife, pulled it right up to Sam's throat, and said a line about leaving his dog alone. Pillars of the community pull out ordinances, dudes pull out knives, but it's the same thing—anything to screw up a dog in the name of some so-called value system that has nothing to do with what a dog is. The dude's idea was that it was wrong to be hard on his dog the way Sam was being, so to avoid moral harm, he pulled his knife. Pillars of the community also get righteous when you have to lay into a dog, preferring to pack dogs into their kindly decompression chambers.

"But Harry is in that class with his Shepherd," Sam said. Harry is a sheriff's officer who likes to work his police dogs with us, and because his dog worked with him in uniform on the beat, he was in uniform in class, gun and all. "I knew he'd be there for me, so I told the dude to take a little look around, and he was looking down the barrel of Harry's .38. I told him to put the bozo toy away and start working his dog, and he did. And damn if that dog and that dude didn't straighten around and start looking alive. Maybe the dog and the dude will both stay out of jail, which is too bad. If Harry weren't such a mean cop, they could both get some kindly counseling." Sam laughed. I did, too, but Luke didn't.

"Morality's wonderful," I said, and then had to deal with Luke, who was worried about the gun, the knife, and so on. I cut him off. "Don't hassle it."

Luke asked Sam if he'd kicked the man with the knife out of class, and Sam said he hadn't, and Luke asked why not.

Sam just said, "Some of these people get straightened out when they train their dogs."

It turned out that there had been some humaniac hecklers shouting at the class, calling the students Nazis because their dogs were on leash and under control, and Sam figured they had raised the tension so that the dude got carried away with the knife routine and a phony notion of his dog's rights. From what Sam said, they'd gotten together on work and movement,

and a different idea of rights was forming. After class the Dobie
owner had stayed to keep working his dog, obviously elevated to
find himself on the same leash with a Dobie moving square and
scopy, the way Dobies do when they're any good at all and lose
interest in behaving like juvenile delinquents.

Luke wanted to know why we couldn't find less public places
than Upfield Park for classes.

Sam said, "A phony trainer finds out about the moral
standards of the community so as to know how high to build the
hedge. A real one finds out where in the community standards
are the most righteous, so as to hold classes there. If you can get
your dog working around in gangland, or on a church lawn on
Sunday morning, you've got a dog who will be there for you,
who can work under fire."

Sam didn't say what I told Luke later that evening when we
were alone, which is that our classes are places where there's
protection for people who want to work their dogs, as well as
places for them to learn how to do it. I said, getting a little
sermony myself, wanting Luke to know this, and pretty proud
of Sam, too. "The born-agains with their guilt weapons, and the
'humane citizens' with their dog-riddance programs that are just
tools to get someone elected to office, and the bad dudes with
their knives, and all the other crooks are in a minority wherever
our classes meet; we see to it that people shape up. That bit with
the knife was over so fast, no one had to know about it; people
got to just go on training their dogs. It's getting worse now, we're
having to go indoors in some places, and it's getting tougher to
fight City Hall, of course, but the classes have to go on. That's
the only place there's any real civility, now that civilization's
getting so noisy."

I could have put that differently, I suppose, but you can get
impatient, so when I said that Luke said that it was pretty
artificial "civility," and I said, of course it was artificial, it was art,
and Luke said you didn't need art for civility, and I said you did

for the kind that makes a dog show up. But that was after Sam told this story.

Luke worried about the knife and the gun again, and said again that he had enough money so that I wouldn't have to teach the classes, I could just work with the dogs I wanted to work with, and so on.

He said, "I know where Sam's coming from, that's what I was doing in the sixties. Trying to make room in the world for life to get larger than the value system that keeps you in the good graces of the Bank of America and which the landscapers of Beverly Hills allows for.

"But you can't take on the world, it'll just take you on instead." I looked at Luke's eyes and saw the clarity and courage there, and thought about his saying that after the hard time Sam and I had given him, and knew what he was offering me.

But I said, "Luke, the dogs don't get trained if me and Sam back off. Especially over in Orange County, where the money and piety are so thick in the air, it's only in our classes a dog can get enough oxygen to retrieve and jump. That's worse than the dude with his knife. And this is why Sam and I are partners. Sam came back from Vietnam, and I came back from the university, thinking there had to be some reality somewhere. . . ."

I tried to go on, to tell Luke how *important* it was, Sam out there putting his body and his reality and his knowledge in between the handlers and dogs and the so-called advantages of America, but Luke was saying that it sounded pretty cynical and that there really were advantages to America, it really was as free as countries get. He was right, but he was wrong, too, and I had no heart, was still too unhappy about failing Sam with the White German Shepherd to point out that, yes, it was a free country for Coca-Cola ads, which were so pretty, no one could see the dogs or anything else. It's hard for someone who doesn't know to get it, about what's at stake with all of those dog-food displays in the supermarkets, and the cute puppies on the commercials, who haven't seen what Sam and I have. Messed up, asymmetrical kids wandering into our classes by accident and learning to walk and talk and love with their dogs once they find an alternative to the deadly, fluffy images. I didn't get it said, because I can't talk, because Sam and I were at odds, anyway, because we didn't have the dog.

At supper that night, Luke, trying to probe against the heaviness that had settled over me and Sam—we could hardly look at each other and couldn't look away, either—asked something about the history of White German Shepherds. Sam delivered himself of a small lecture on the uselessness of such questions when you're commissioned by Hollywood to find a good one.

"But what are they for?" asked Luke.

"They aren't for anything, and God only knows what the breeders think they're doing," Sam said.

"What are their origins?"

"They don't have any origins!" I said sharply.

Then I softened, thanks to Luke staying as courteous as Homer ever could, and explained that the white ones are normally culled, and rambled on for a while until I came to mention that even in Border Collies, too much white is frowned on because it horrifies the sheep. Luke woke up at this. "So the sheep know?"

"Know what?"

"White is the color of death."

Sam was interested in this but said, "Well, yes, but that doesn't explain how come sheep aren't horrified by sheep, then. Sheep are white, you know. Maybe it's just that a white dog looks too much like a sheep, and it scares them the way monkeys scare people, or the way ponies and mules and donkeys scare horses. Maybe a white dog looks like a travesty of a sheep."

Luke thought about this and said, "Well, maybe for a sheep the white of a dog's coat just isn't a very realistic form of white."

Sam nodded in acknowledgment of what Luke said, a slow tilt of his serious, bearlike head. Luke didn't see it.

I thought of Samoyeds like George, herding reindeer. But reindeer aren't sheep, and Samoyeds aren't German Shepherds.

Sam went off then—to see Jenny?—and Homer appeared to prefer to stay on the rug, resting, so we took just Prince out to run a bedtime check on the kennels. There was a good moon, and we didn't need the kennel lights. We had a Deerhound boarding with us, Millie, who had come along so fast, I agreed when Luke asked if she couldn't be let out, and you would have had a hard time improving on the picture she made, graceful as a legend in the moonlight. Luke went into one run where there was an entrancingly attractive and feisty little Cairn Terrier, about Prince's size, to medicate one of the Cairn's ears. Luke had taken to the game little dog, and enjoyed tending him. The Cairn was not the sort of dog to be dedicated to escaping, but he didn't like the medicine and managed to wiggle away from Luke and come streaking out, to dance around, yipping happily. Before we knew what else was happening, he and Prince both had taken up field positions and were dancing within inches of each other, a rumbling war dance.

The Deerhound had been about a hundred feet away, trailing something, and then she was standing between the two contenders like a queen. She gave each of them a slow look, not menacing, but not inviting in its aristocractic evaluation, either. Both Prince and the Cairn remembered to worry about fleas, abashed to have behaved so around royalty, and the Deerhound lay down quietly between them, her eyes gentle but commanding, and the incident was over that gracefully; Homer couldn't have done it better.

As we walked back, in the state of awe one is in when beauty like the Deerhound's happens to nudge you in just that way. I said, "There can't be more happiness than knowing such things as that."

Luke said, "Then why are you and Sam both still anxious

about finding another dog? You've already done it here at the kennel, you've got a world in which dogs live in a fullness of being. . . . I walked into your class with a pet Sheltie, and now I have Prince, a partner, with all of his reality visible—all of the thought in his bones and hide that I'd never even guessed at. You're living in a vision already. Why are you still searching? How could a movie matter so much?"

"Because it would mean something if it were shown just right, even for a few frames, in a movie, and it is my happiness and Sam's to care about that, and I'm anxious because you still haven't *heard* me about what we let go when I lost that dog. There won't be another like him."

Luke said—Luke was right and I was right and this was no wrangle—"But happiness is just life coming to us, to anyone, in the parts where death and pain and hatred are left out, and will you marry me? Take me as your lawfully wedded husband?"

We were both startled. I thought about how Luke's love and intelligence got right into me, and I thought about what deep comfort it would be to marry him, to shore up what I already had, and wanted to say yes, but the movie and finding the dog and remembering the dog I could have had—all this had to happen first, and I wasn't sure you could just shore up what you had, in any case.

"Luke, you don't know yet if you can make a life here in the kennel. You know you don't like things like the knife incident last night—is this a life you want?"

"If you married me, you wouldn't have to—"

I interrupted him. "I have to. The *dust* around here is valuable."

"Is dust necessary to dog training?" He was upset, so I snuggled against him instead of replying, hoping it would go away, thinking, If only he could see. Luke was right about his happiness, probably, but we have all been flung loose, flung loose, like that Shepherd, making all his own meaning at Skef-fington's, and life wasn't just going to come to us, or anyway, the kind that does isn't my happiness. Some said that we've all been to Vietnam, and that isn't true, but something like it is, and it happens at birth: Things like Vietnam just announce it to us, if you need that kind of announcement.

Luke, his arms around me, had to ask, "Is there something wrong with safety?"

I lied, saying, "No, of course not." But there is, if you're nagged by infinitude and have seen it in a dog.

Seven
HOMER
AND I
SEARCH
NORTHWARD

One day soon there was another exchange between Luke and Sam, a tense one. Luke was working Prince, Sam was working the little English Cocker, and I was working Homer. Working Homer had become my self-granted reward for getting honorably through the bread-and-butter training of the day.

There were rules that Luke just didn't know, and he asked Sam, right out, "Sam, how come you don't have a dog of your own?"

Sam looked up from Martha, the English Cocker. They were taking a breather, and Martha was checking out Sam's fingers, which Sam was allowing her to do.

"I train dogs all day long. What do I need a dog for?"

Luke said, "I thought—well, the same reason anybody else does. I was remembering when I got Prince for Esther—there were already plenty of dogs, and . . ." He looked from Sam to me, but I couldn't wrangle even a faint smile in the tension, and I gathered from the silence that Sam was having trouble, too, as though Luke had inadvertently wandered into a mine field that might get us all.

Sam wouldn't say it, I thought, but he did. "Luke, how come you're just writing human-interest features for the desert edition of the *Herald*?"

Luke said, "I told Diane . . ."

Sam said, "Annie—Diane—and I are *training* dogs." Sam didn't look at me, because we both knew Sam was refusing Luke's question, just as Luke's question was refusing Sam. "But we're still training dogs. Why aren't you writing?"

Luke said, with nervous resentment. "My writing killed a man, got people hurt."

Sam was silent, then more gentle. "Okay. My training killed a valley. People, birds, flowers, rodents, snakes. Even the leeches. Dogs, too, maybe. So you live and learn better. But you have to live if you're going to learn better," Sam added.

But Sam still wasn't living with a dog, which was why I was doing most of the looking for the White German Shepherd, and why it had turned out that there was a kind of silent agreement that I was to do the training on this dog, if we ever found it. Ever since Zeus died, Sam hadn't had another dog, and furthermore, he had quietly backed away from every situation in which he might be in any danger of getting another dog. But it hadn't been up to Luke to challenge. Luke's question made my ribs hurt with loyalty to Sam, loyalty to Luke, too, but loyalty to Sam was in me like knowledge, like my knowledge of a well-bent stifle. I was lost in loyalty to Luke, unable to say what Sam had said to him, and afraid that I would lose my breath in Luke's fragility. Then I lost it, remembering that Luke was on our turf here at the kennel, but . . .

There is something piercingly horrible about the death of a good working dog, not worse than other piercingly horrible things but very specific. In Sam's case, still specific to Zeus, I thought. Sam has demons. The demons of dog trainers—Sam and me, anyway, are black and deep and sticky, and if you have a dog of your own, they can put buckets of grief in your way as you move with your dog, and it can turn out that the more you want to work your own dog, the more grief there is to trip over. Sam met some demons in Vietnam, too, in addition to the usual ones, because he had learned that greatness can mean biting into the knowledge of death, and once that's happened, that's what it is, unless you clear a different sort of space for it. Movies instead of wars. And Sam wouldn't put it this way, but he can't help the genius that comes into his handling, and he can't help knowing what some dogs can do by way of response to that, and the demons tell him everything. Luke had maybe gotten a glimpse of that and dodged for the ranch. Sam just kept on knowing.

But that isn't the only thing to know, there's also ordinary happiness to make with training, especially in the teaching, and Sam's demons leave him alone when he works other people's dogs, since that situation is already artificial enough to obscure the knowledge of how deeply you can and will fail a great-hearted dog, and if it is your own dog and great-hearted—and the dog couldn't help but be great-hearted if it was Sam's dog—then the demons would jitter-jitter-jitter death at Sam, the demons knowing that Kipling had only half of it, with that poem about how dogs tear your heart when they die. The dogs give their hearts to us to tear, too, and it is a dog trainer's business to be ready for a dog's heart. Sam wasn't just afraid of his own grief.

Luke said, "I'm living, and I know what I want!"

Sam looked at Luke for a moment or two—I wish he hadn't—looked at Luke knowing everything, everything.

Luke was asymmetrical but still shining, perfect. I was blinded, but when Luke started to say something else, I said, "Luke! Leave it!" He turned and walked away, back to my cottage to, as I learned later, change and go out on an interview. I wanted to follow, terrified to lose him but terrified to lose me, too, if I did.

Sam said, "Time for some coffee."

In his cottage, at his kitchen table, we had coffee. In his cottage Sam told me, "Jenny's out of it, Annie. And I'm tired. Maybe I ought to be a monk." His eyes were red and wet. I thought that maybe this time it hadn't been Sam who kept the woman out of the kennel. Jenny had done the breaking off, I knew—it had happened before, and twice Sam had tried again. "She wanted me to move in with her. Treat the kennel like a regular business now that we have help." He closed his eyes and then said, "Ah, hell. Let's go get some paint, put Freddie to work on the kennel office."

So that's what we did.

Within a month we learned even more how hard it was going to be to find a White German Shepherd. We drove in to see Jack Kaye a couple of times, not to show him any dogs because there weren't any dogs to show, but rather to talk—or to hear *him* talk—about how it had to be the right dog.

There was a woman with a kennel above San Francisco who had twenty black-and-tan Shepherds and half again as many white ones—odd for her to have both. I forget how we got her name, but we called her up and told her what we needed, and she said that she had it, two or three dogs with the size, color, pigmentation and, especially, temperament.

"Thirty dogs," Sam said. "There has to be *something*."

I could have flown up, but by this time I was liking the driving around with Homer, so I packed a bag and some camping equipment, Homer stuffed himself in the back of the Toyota, I hitched up the dog trailer, and we set out at dusk to avoid the daytime heat.

We used Homer once in a bad film based vaguely on *The Hound of the Baskervilles*. This was ridiculous, since a sound Irish Wolfhound is about as ferocious as an English country vicar in a civilized murder mystery. Homer is many other fine things, though, including good company on a trip. He doesn't guard the car when I'm not in it—like most Wolfhounds, he has an underdeveloped sense of private property—but he's wonderful for protecting one's person, not that it comes up much once anyone has seen a detail or so of Homer's efficiently rangy self. People don't want to press an issue with him or me once they get a good, or even a blurred, look.

Homer has *temperament.*

You need temperament for police work and war, and for hunting, and for what used to be called real life, which here means things that don't happen much in real life these days in America. And you need temperament for art, which includes movies. In a movie, if the director listens, you can use the whole dog, yourself, too, and no bloodshed. Homer is the tallest temperament anyone ever gets to see.

So as Homer and I pulled out of some little town, I would grin like a fool, remembering the small exchanges I had with people when they saw Homer in the back of the tiny car, and sometimes the things I had to say to keep gas-station attendants calm, not that Homer barked at them. People liked to say, "Why don't you save gas, have him pull the car?" And I liked to answer, "Forty miles per hour is his top speed, no good for freeways."

Of course, they also asked, "Does he bite?" There is no right answer to that question, because it is a fake question. I had to do attack work with Homer because when you're looking for lost kids on the posse, you sometimes find situations that are less than benign, but the dog has real brains, doesn't get his kicks bothering people or scaring them, so I almost always replied, "No," even when "Yes" was a better answer, and Homer would arrange himself to look as much as he could like a mild-mannered reporter, settling his square gray jaw into an appealingly naïve expression.

We drove north from Jurupa, through the Cajon Pass, across the Mojave Desert where the Joshua trees stuck up as they do, looking almost like humans, some of them. The Mormons had named them, thinking that they looked like Joshua leading them into the promised land. I don't know that it was necessarily that, but the Mojave has its explicit mysteries. Then we crossed the Tehachapi Pass and down into Bakersfield where we made a pit stop. The attendant was a hostile jerk, so when he asked, "Does he bite?" I said, "Only at night," and the attendant, who was fattish and red-faced, turned his pious eyes away from my boobs and considered Homer instead, nervously trying to figure out if he could get back inside the office before an angry Wolfhound could get out of a Toyota.

We drove on in the deadness of three A.M., leaving behind the central valley where agribusiness has been claiming the deserts that used to be murals that rewarded several lifetimes of any length of study. These deserts, sometimes, are the cosmos. This night, however, the west side of the central valley, not yet left behind, was simply a hot place without water, and for us, even driving at night, the task was never to get any thirstier than you have to. That night the roominess of the desert was also a warning to creatures from almost anywhere else to plan their way carefully.

Once I drove to Las Vegas from Jurupa in the summer, during the day, with a dog. I let the dog out to run at one point—he was a pup, a German Shorthair, with nothing much in his head as yet and wired up, "birdy." He ran in circles, and then I gave him all of the inadequate supply of drinking water I had in the car, and a few miles later the car boiled over—every drop boiled out of the radiator as if driven by a curse—and there I was, broken down, with a hot dog who had the basal metabolism of a shooting star, and no one came by, and he died after three hours and a bit.

You have to remember what a dog is, what a car is, what a desert is. We were thirty minutes from water—at seventy miles per hour.

I buried the pup and waited in rock shade until, at around

nightfall, a car stopped and helped. I wanted the pup to have been a great dog, one of the greatest field-trial dogs of all time— you can think what you like, you know, once the dog is in the ground—but his shoulders were just a bit straight despite a noble ancestry. He would have been fine for what we wanted him for, which was to play the part of a great field-trial dog in a movie version of *Brag Dog*. The film didn't get made.

The drive with Homer went well. No trouble, and we got to pull over the Golden Gate Bridge before the sun was truly and completely risen. It was cool in the city and downright chilly out on the bridge, where Homer recognized the fog.

Homer was bred to a gray wisdom almost as ancient as the fog itself, bred with alert eyes that took him through it in a companionable awareness even though this was the first real fog he had seen. His hide remembered, and when we came to the bridge and its revelations, Homer whined in greeting.

On the north side of the bridge, I pulled over so we could get out and look across the small amount of the bay we could see, or guess at, which was just about none at all; the fog was too thick, even with the sun seeming to be nearly risen. Homer stood with his paws on the cement guard beside me and panted, in and out, the odd, foggy air. With him standing like that, his shoulders were the height of my head. I leaned against him, and both of us, sleepy after the night drive, dreamed into the now thinning swirls.

After a few minutes Homer indicated with a sigh that he was finished with the bridge, and we walked back to the car and kept going north on 101.

Snocote Kennel, with its thirty White German Shepherds, was not far now, just the other side of breakfast. And suddenly there it was, where the golden hills of Marin County begin, and there was the new fencing and the impeccable landscaping and the kennel cleaned three times a day and the Winnebago beside the kennel, kept for attending dog shows—not licensed ones— and there was the tanned, athletic lady, and there were the dogs.

Pretty enough if you squinted and didn't look right at them, but tentative, with no spring behind, no angulation in front, no substance in the backs, and if there were backs, there was no continuation of substance to the head and neck.

For me there is no prettiness to speak of in dogs; beauty is as beauty does. But the slender, competent-looking woman saw *type*, where I saw an orthopedic and psychic nightmare, or at least a bad dream. A "typy" dog is one that approaches some platonic ideal of that breed, but most of the people who talk about "type" forget that we only see it as shadows most of the time, and we see it clearest when a dog is *doing* something, not when we stare over their heads. I see type in work, not in poses for photographers, not that there's anything wrong with photography. These dogs didn't have a purpose, a job to do. Their minds were already crippled and squirrelly, and their bodies would be too arthritic to support them before they were in what should be their primes, most of them. They were trash. God forgive the people who do this to dogs. I can't forgive them, it's not my business to do so.

Homer and I drove some more, seeing the countryside, and later found a small campground slightly farther north, where it was quiet enough to sleep in the daytime. The place was heavy with blackberries, as though someone with an old-style Hollywood idea of set decor had draped the sweet stuff all over, like edible velvet for Cleopatra. I knew I should sleep before starting back, but I spent some time standing with Homer, eating blackberries and about ready to give up on the dog and the movie. I couldn't think worth a damn, and I said, "Some dog trainer you, Diane! You wore that shirt, not because it's handy for trips with all of the pockets but because it's the softest shirt you own, and the point about the shirt is how your breasts look under the checks, how Luke's hands would feel touching it, how quickly and smoothly you could unsnap it while kissing Luke's throat."

I forgot entirely that if Luke had been with me, I would have had to apologize for saying "trash," or refrain from saying it, forgot that if I did, I would have to tell him the gory details of what comes of random sentiments for dogs, and instead I thought I'd like to buy a swirly, clinging knit jersey dress and wear it out somewhere with Luke. Denims and a shirt are two things to take off. A dress would be just one. A dress you could just pull up. Not that it was sex, exactly, but that Luke's body was a picture of what I loved. Then the thought of the white dog who had to be as good as the one I had turned away nudged my thoughts and, a little later, my rags of dreams in which I didn't find the dog forever.

I spent most of my sleeping time mooning and worrying, and it was nearly sunset before my mind let me go, so Homer and I stayed there that night, after I drove in to call Luke and Sam and say I would be a day late. Luke was out, interviewing. Sam agreed to leave him a note, in case he came in to sleep at the kennel that night.

Homer slept beside me, and though he doesn't cuddle, couldn't actually cuddle, he can sleep as close as cashmere when necessary, which allowed me to sleep, and as I drifted off I kept thinking about That Dog, the one now guarding discarded distributor heads and radiators, though I knew that this meant I would be thinking about him when I woke up instead of how to find the dog we could use.

I thought about Luke, too, knowing that I would wake in his case as well to the thoughts I went to sleep with, and got cross with him and reminded myself that Luke's life had never really had anything to do with kennels—I imagine the cattle dogs slept with their cowboys—and it wasn't his fault, but with such a man, if I'm not careful, my Irish Wolfhound and my whole life could lose its chance to be an activity of love's most ancient knowledge and become instead, what-are-we-going-to-do-with-the-dog?

Why didn't I fall in love with a dog trainer? A friend asked me once when I was still young enough to think that talking about contradictions made them better for me, and I said that there weren't so many of them as you might think, for one thing, not the kind that can love precisions for their own sakes. And there are even fewer who were bearable. Sam was the only one I could stand to have around for any length of time because he was like me, only quieter, and male.

Sam only had a year of college, a year more than most trainers, but his father came from Yorkshire—Sam's got horses as well as dogs in his blood—and married an American woman who was there in connection with the war in some way and moved with her to New York and raised horses and lectured at Cornell, I think, on artificial insemination in the draft breeds. They call it capsule breeding.

That's all I know about Sam's father, except that his name was Joe Carraclough. I don't know how he came to be a horseman from Yorkshire who went to Oxford—did I mention that?—but that's what he was. He didn't raise and train dogs after he came to America, so Sam discovered all of that the same way I did, when he was just about done growing up, and then he had more experience in Vietnam and that one year of college.

I went to college, too, and was going to paint because my mother used to buy books and read them, and I got the idea of making something like a poem or a painting, but I wasn't any good at painting. Not good enough, anyway—and somehow by then I was training dogs. I had always liked to train them, but I mean, I started Being a Dog Trainer, which is not the same thing and may not be as good, and I met Sam at a tracking trial, and we became partners.

And now I was looking for what might or might not be an actual dog somewhere, though so far, all that had happened was I passed by the right dog, the one that could stand twice as big as life, making finely accurate judgments about Skeffington's customers and about Mrs. Skeffington too. I had passed by the right dog and needed another one that would be right.

Eight
RETURN

I slept long enough and quietly enough to wake a little stiff. Homer was lying beside me. You never saw such a dog for consideration in the morning, and canine common sense, too, waiting for you to get up at your own pace so that dreams and philosophy will linger with you there, on the edge of sleep for a while.

He looked at me quietly and stretched his head and neck up for a moment, gently enough so that I could watch and stroke while remembering my last dream, of Luke looking grave and happy, and then I started, dangerously, thinking how much better breakfast would be with him there to split the bacon with, but I recovered quickly enough, fed Homer, had two cups of coffee and repacked the car.

I had a whole day to kill before it would be cool enough to hit the inland road back south, or I could use the day taking the coast route. I stayed there, working out how to drift around a little, which, because I was still tired, meant finding a coffee shop once I got up to Santa Rosa where there was one fairly like the ones I was used to, in the South. I ate breakfast reading the *San Francisco Chronicle,* finding no Shepherds of any color advertised and thinking how good a writer Luke was.

I rechecked the classifieds under "Pets," for White German Shepherds, found nothing, and did the same with the Santa Rosa paper and the smaller local ones. I even put my own notice cards in two pet stores and the feed-and-tack shops I could find, places where the cards will yellow faster than dust, as they are covered by ads for the stud services of registered Arabians and Anglo-Hanoverian horses or whatever other cross someone is working with.

This at least served to distract me from thinking full-time about Luke's eyes, gray with amber-sharp and amber-mellow streaks of gold in them. I never saw such eyes before.

In the late afternoon I found, in Cotati, a café with a good menu, grass behind it for Homer to stretch his paws in, and a refugee musician from San Francisco who sang folk songs in a pleasingly scholarly, accurate and heartrending way. Then I was back on the road at last, the two beers I had had working with me, making me just restless enough, right for being on the road, awake, wanting urgently to get over the bridge, down the peninsula and find Highway 5 at last stretching long and straight in front of me, better than any song for thinking long and straight.

The timing was right, and I was well south of San Francisco by eight P.M., feeling the familiar grab of cabin fever as the highway flowed by, and I anticipated happily the long night, including even the fatigue that would come. Driving on Highway 5, I can be half awake, half dreaming, half thinking and still watching the road, and it's best with Homer there to think with me or to think his own thoughts, so that my dreams are pulled up more gently into consciousness than I can do by myself, and so with less damage.

I was dreaming about the movie, seeing a dog, white in the snow, bounding through snowdrifts the way I thought snowdrifts themselves bounded when I was a child and had never seen snow. Seeing a man clumsy with clothes and equipment, but his clumsiness no offense to the snow because of the dog. When there is such a dog, then there are the two of them, human and dog, with what Jack London calls love tricks akin to hurt, the dog biting the man softly, and the man cursing the dog even more softly, and both of them knowing the bites and curses for love: The wilderness knows when you let it choose you, instead of your trying to choose it. This redeems the man as though the wilderness forgave him, which the wilderness will never do, but a good dog is born as clean as a wolf. The wilderness is different when the dog comes, as long as the man doesn't fall in love with a city woman, of course; Jack London doesn't say anything about that.

There was the highway, and me and Homer driving right down the whole length of it, accompanied by the idea of this dog I am looking for. Over and over again I saw this: the White German Shepherd, full of it, ready to go. The knowledge of that possibility is prior to the knowledge of love. At least I could think that for a while, isolated in my car with Homer and the road.

Nine

A DOG
BITE
AND A
BAD FIT

When I got home, Freddie was observing Baron, a Mastiff who was learning to be still, while he evaluated the passing traffic of children going to school, and Sam had already fed the dogs and was hosing out the runs, so he had been up early—it was only a quarter to six. I was exhausted as I pulled in and could think of nothing but coffee and bed. Bed wasn't possible, but coffee and some chatter with Sam was a good consolation. I worked behind him, using the squeegee after he hosed, watering and replacing one automatic waterer that had broken.

Sam looked as tired as I felt, or more, not even replacing the big hose on its wheel, and I was so tired that I didn't notice it until we were already at the table and Homer nudged me firmly enough to make me look out the window and check things over again. I went out and coiled it up. Homer, that bit of duty taken care of, lay down near the table, groaning a bit with fatigue, too, but mostly with a happy, undisturbed relaxation.

Sam said nothing about the fact that I came home with an empty dog trailer. I said what the dogs had been, and Sam said, "Yeah, well, the breeders hold their dogs still and look at them, and there's no dog there. Nobody can see a dog who's standing still, nobody has that kind of character."

"Including you and me, Sam."

He thought that over, nodded and said, "Baron took the rag yesterday."

This was a relief. We were agitating Baron for a local police department. He had novice obedience, retrieving and a little tracking based on the retrieving, but he had been slow to alert on suspicious people, much less grab hard enough and fast enough to take the rag away from Sam. He was a pretty good dog, but unfortunately he was only loaned to the P.D. rather than owned by them. The kennel wouldn't ask for him back—it was advertising for them, but a cop's dog should be that cop's dog, on the paperwork and everywhere. Baron hadn't been assigned to an officer yet, which was another thing that was going to go wrong with this dog program if they didn't give the cop time to work the dog in and out.

Agitation is attack work, or man work. You need a skillful handler to play the heavy—the burglar, murderer or whatever—convincingly while making the right moves. In effect, the agitator systematically teases a dog so that he becomes highly suspicious of people whose manner, movements and/or voice betray that they are somewhere they ought not to be and know it. At first the "thug" retreats if the dog so much as stares in his direction. The more confident the dog, the more aggravating the heavy's actions, until the dog goes for him, growls or barks. There is a great deal more to it than this, and it won't work without the great deal more, but "taking the rag" means a significant move forward in Baron's work. We had been worried about Baron, not because he was timid or anything like it, but because he wasn't very suspicious and was slow to get worried in the kind of situation where a police dog ought to be worried. Now he'd learned that there really was such a thing as a human varmint, which meant he'd probably do fine. Later, watching him work, we saw that it was all there, solid gold.

I thought of Sam sometimes as one of the few people in this world to get his head all the way around the idea that a police dog or a sentry dog or a personal-protection dog is supposed to love people. Heart and courage are what a police dog thinks with. Would you lay down your life or even risk pain for someone you hated? Dogs are not basically different from us in this way, except that they are more forgiving than most humans are.

While my mind was wandering to general issues, Sam had hunched deeper over his coffee and finally said the obvious. I had been hoping for a way around this conversation and what it might lead to. Sam too.

"No dogs up there, huh?"

"There wasn't even anything that looked like a distant relative of a dog, or no dog I would ever name Dog. So what do we do now? Maybe we ought to forget the whole damn project and just build up more local business, put in the new runs and clean up the empty pasture for hurdles, and quit thinking like wandering starlets."

Sam made a low, noncommittal noise and stared at an imaginary and apparently very detailed object halfway between his coffee cup and mine.

I did about the same. There were other reasons to be gloomy besides the nonexistent White German Shepherd. I was specifically not looking forward to working Lion (full name, Lion Smoke), a big chunky cross between an Airedale and some kind of Southern big-game dog, who wasn't very big on human-ity. I was feeling she was the sort of dog no one deserves more than one of in a lifetime, no matter how sleazily you run your mind or your training kennel. Lion seemed to have studied human anatomy carefully, and she wasn't going to miss.

The sourness didn't feel inborn in her, and I didn't know what had been going on for her before she came to our kennel, but the nerve-racking part was wondering how deeply the rational animal was buried in her. I was not afraid of her, but the thing is, you put all of that work—and in this case both Sam and I doing it—into that kind of dog and you're still probably not going to have much when you're done. Chances were she would always need professional handling.

Sam did most of the handling, and I helped largely by doing a lot of what isn't, with a good dog, that much time and trouble—trying to teach her that there were people in the world who were *not* human varmints. I played the part of the innocent passerby, something Lion had no idea of yet, and I would soon take over the leash so that she would learn to accept, not formal commands but simple contact with people besides Sam.

Later that day when we worked Lion, Luke was out with us, preparing gallant little Prince to try out for a relay team. He and Prince had gotten respectably high scores in regular obedience trials, and he wanted to branch out, try something new with his dog. He was also talking about getting other enthusiasts for a scent-hurdle team, which Sam and I would have to handle together for a little bit.

Freddie's Blue looked like the fastest dog we would have. Homer liked such work, but the hurdles, set for smaller dogs, were too close together for him to get up his full speed. It took more than the whole length of the hurdles, plus the scent platform, for Homer to find his huge stride, but he seemed to like to sit back watching, getting excited when his friends were in the lead.

Prince was being too daring and feisty, irreverently growling and prancing his way over the hurdles and back as if it were a musical-comedy routine rather than a racing form he was learning, tossing the dumbbell in the air and catching it with half-pretend ferocity as a way of announcing his pleasure in having his mettle tried. Scent hurdles are not like regular competitions in which any noises, mumbles, burps or snatches of song from the dog are penalized, but such sideshow antics destroy speed and concentration, so when Luke, instead of correcting Prince, threw back his head and laughed, standing there with a staunch little dog he could do anything with if only he'd save the laughter until the end of the run, I lost my temper. If I hadn't been so afraid of losing him, I would have established the rules calmly a long time ago and let him make his choice, but I'd dallied, worried all the time about what was compatible with the vision of Esther, and now I swore at Luke in a steady, sharp way, the way Ahab sometime cursed the ocean and the whale.

"That goddamn does it!" from me brought from Luke only an amiably puzzled look—"What does what?" his eyes asked—and I couldn't explain my sense that the cosmos was watching this part of the passage of time, and that allowing people, especially Luke, to mess around like that with good dogs at my kennel was one way to inspire the air to fog and swirl like dust after mirages, obscuring the dog I wanted, obscuring training—betraying, really, everything—and if people like Luke wouldn't let their Shelties mess up over the hurdles, there wouldn't have to be those thirty or so White German Shepherds up there in Novato, swaying crookedly over no terrain.

Then Prince had a go at jumping a hurdle sideways, and Luke laughed again. Fury flooded me. I went back to Lion, who miraculously hadn't tried anything during this small episode, though I had been on the other end of her leash all of this time. I turned to her, off-balance, and commanded her to "Stay!" as though I had a right to. The sound of the phony command—subtly but unmistakably different to the ears of a dog who has learned to be aware of it—pushed her criminal-dog-crazy-belligerence button, and she lunged murderously, not for me but for the nearest human being besides me—in this case Luke. I automatically shouted while reaching to jerk her off her feet and let her feel the end of the world there for a little bit, but my striking back must have been too slow; she was already following my hands back in the direction of the correction when the training collar, by some fluke, slipped off her neck as Lion followed through on her lunge, all ninety pounds of socially maldeveloped canine, and got on my arm.

Any dog bite hurts like thunder, because the shape of a dog's teeth causes a lot of deep bruising. And this bite started as puncture wounds and became two rips down my arm as well, tearing what felt like assorted tendons but actually was only one, in my hand, and there was the fat poking out of the punctures like a new, dreadful kind of mutant worm.

That's how Luke would describe it later, anyway, but that is no reason to judge him. The dogs were going to do the judging that needed doing, and Luke was going to know it in a way he needn't have. I would be judged, too, but I had chosen dogs.

As this was happening, I grabbed with my left hand for my tranquilizer (a wooden dowling covered with rubber so it doesn't break any bones—a safety club, you might say). This was a moment when I didn't give as much of a hoot as I usually do about the dog's safety, but it was a very tiny instant, and I have myself too well trained to stop for that kind of emotion, so I grabbed the tranq even before she had loosened up to find a better grip, and thumped her on the nose.

Tough as Lion was and wanted to be, she wasn't accustomed to sudden pain of that sort. She staggered back in a brief fireworks of confusions—she was a novice, thank God, so by the time she lunged again, I had managed to get the leash under control, using mostly my left arm, and used it, two-handed now, as a kind of lasso to catch the dog and hold her for a few seconds.

All of this took maybe six or seven seconds, which gave Sam time to sprint from the door of the kennel to the training area and grab the leash before my hold on it with my one usable arm collapsed.

As soon as Sam had the leash, my arm won out in its efforts to convince me that it couldn't, shouldn't, be asked to do anything at all, so I let it hang for a moment as though it were paralyzed, then held it up to try to keep the bleeding and pain down. I was too zonked for a moment or two even to use my good left hand to hold the hurt arm up. I finally got that, too, and leaned back on the fence and gave myself to watching Sam bash Lion around for a while and think that I had again learned more than I wanted to about my own responses to various kinds of pain.

Dog trainers are supposed to correct dogs, not punish them, and Sam is no punisher, but it may have been that he came down on the dog more times than was really necessary to get her to walk sedately at heel, back to her run.

Coming back, Sam let loose with rage, not at the dog but at Luke: "Where the goddamn hell were you? Why didn't you help her? Why aren't you on your way to the hospital? Where are the fucking tourniquets?"

Luke looked like a man just coming around from a near knockout blow in round eight, and it may not even have registered with him that there had been a bite until Sam let loose.

Sam knows as well as I do that people who aren't used to animal work—and I mean by that more than just training one, two or three household pets—often just don't see injuries or understand them, not being used to the speed of the revenge biology can take on the thoughtless craftsmen of creatures. Luke wasn't an idiot, after all, though when he came out of his brief trance, and I had to deal with his endearing but inept Florence Nightingale responses, he was a pain in the neck, and that was on top of the injured arm. The bite hurt worse and worse as the seconds ticked by.

I didn't mind if it healed with scars and was happy to use whiskey as a painkiller and nerve-settler, but I wasn't strong enough to battle Luke's anxieties. I had to tell him what to do, and mostly what not to do, and agreed to go along to the emergency room where it was well into the wee hours before we were done. I was X-rayed, stitched and bandaged and, best of all, my mind was gently swaddled in Demerol, so I felt no immediate need to combat the airtight argument Luke was constructing about my giving up dog training. I remembered his laughter when Prince mouthed off over the jumps, and thought for a moment, Yes, you could lose yourself in that laughter. Luke's laughter is as noble and open as sunlight.

Later, though, when we were back home and settled in the living room, I heard in his voice the sound of arguments with too much history to them, as though we had been married and eating away at the temples of each other's hearts for years.

When my arm started to speak up again, I became just about as intolerant as you can get.

"You say that dog is never going to be much good, anyway. So why do you have to train dogs like that, then? It's sick, it's suicidal," Luke said, and he added. "Or maybe you shouldn't train dogs at all. Maybe you are just too physically slight for this kind of work as a constant thing."

Mercifully for my conscience, I don't remember what I said in reply; my clearest memory, after the bite, is of Homer on the drive home, in the backseat with Luke at the wheel, doing one of his wicked (if you ask me), though fortunately rare, clown tricks. That night he kept reaching with one paw to touch the car window, then pulling back with a shriek—not a metaphorical shriek, you know, but a Wolfhound one—then whimpering and holding out his injured paw to Luke every few minutes.

Luke kept reaching back to pat Homer and worrying, and I don't think he tumbled to it the whole of that ride, although later he claimed he saw through it instantly and was only trying indirectly to soothe me, who didn't need much soothing then. He laughed when he claimed this, laughed at Homer laughing at him, and I thought, bemused, of Homer actually clowning with Luke. Two tall ones, giants at play.

Three days later my arm still hurt, though less, plus Luke was still pushing his line about give-up-the-risks, though he had gotten over the touchy part of things rather quickly and was now compounding his misdeeds by offering reasonable alternatives to dog training, especially alternatives that involved my leaving the kennel to live with him and my not having to worry about money, only training dogs I really wanted to train, and only for people who really deserved them.

You don't build kennels and learn how to train dogs by listening to that kind of advice—cautious, sensible and generous as it may have been—and I wondered, anyway, what he thought I would do with my time then.

"So, then I will have time to knit, sew and cook for you? And get advice on the best polish to use on rosewood?"

As soon as I'd said this—no, before I even knew I was going to say it—I knew we would all, especially me, have been better off if I hadn't said it. I was aggravated to find that Luke found it completely mystifying. He got more and more mystified, so that I doubted what I'd thought and wondered if I'd made it up about the rosewood table and the fresh flowers and was on the point of making a little list of the things I was sorry about until Luke's jaw became grim and large.

"At least don't work that hellhound, Lion. Let Sam do that."

Thank heavens he said that. Now I could quit being sorry. "Look, the goddamn collar came off by a sheer fluke. It wasn't because I am short, or a woman, or anything. It could have happened to Davy Crockett. It's just a thing that can happen, like leaks in brake lines."

"Just a thing that can happen! What it is, is something that happens to people who think they have to prove themselves when there is nothing they have to prove, especially not by wrestling a psychopathic, half-bred bitch. . . ."

"*I* am at least only half-bred and a bitch and maybe psycho-pathic. . . ."

"Wrestle crazy animals and make up tall tales about what it all means. . . ."

"You who've turned from everything you've been committed to are asking me to marry you?"

It got so bad that Luke wrote some poems. They were good, but he knew better, and he would laugh at the cliché of it, showing them to me, and I would laugh, too, but we couldn't laugh it off. One had a line in it about being "plagued by this informed goddess," which was supposed to be a compliment, but who wants to be a plague, and I asked him what in the world he *wanted*, for chrissake? And I meant to make my voice go up some with humor but didn't.

He gave me no answer, of course, or rather dozens of un-answers—whoever does give an answer to such a question uttered in such circumstances?—but Luke apologized for the poem's having upset me and said that he should have known better. That he did know better. And I apologized and said that there was nothing to know better than, and that it was a good poem. But none of us knew anything at that point. We didn't know worse, and we didn't know better.

■

Including Sam, who one day soon after the failed excursion north and the dog bite went crashing around the kennel, swearing like a sailor rather than a dog trainer. I could have taken comfort from this but demanded of him, as I had of Luke, what the goddamn hell was wrong, what did he want?

"It's my life!" This he said in the general direction of my hurt arm and the wall, interrupting himself from folding some clean bedding from the drier. The office-cum-grooming room smelled agreeably of kennel wash and clean dog, and I took a deep breath of it for reassurance.

"What's wrong with your life?"

Sam's reply surprised me as much as anything I've ever heard. He said, "It's *inconvenient*, that's what!"

Here he picked up a water bucket and started banging it violently against the wall, over and over, like in a movie about mental patients. Then he stopped and examined the bucket, which was now crumpled, looking bemused, as though he hadn't any idea why the bucket was in his hand.

"Look at it! Look at what a damn inconvenient mess this bucket is! This—this place—looks like what it virtually is, a movie set about a street gang that someone decided to try calling a kennel. It's not even a set for a kennel but for a damn hideout!"

"You're quoting someone, Sam. It's a good kennel."

"Yeah. The kennel's okay, Annie." This he said at the beginning of a sob. Then he followed through on the sob after a moment of stop-action. Sam's grief usually shows more clearly and less noisily—he sobbed quietly, but that he sobbed at all was the wonder.

I actually put my arms around him, for the first time since Zeus died, unless you count greetings and farewell hugs connected with difficult competitions and long journeys, and I said, "Ah, Sam, it's going to be okay, Sam," and Sam simply went soft and slid down the wall to the floor, me following and still hanging on for I don't know how long, maybe an hour, without speaking, because the sun was setting and the dogs had fully recovered from their dismay at Sam's outburst and were speaking about feeding time. So we got up, cold and stiff, me feeling as though my whole mind and body, all the wherewithal to hold a leash or a lover instead of just my arm, had been chewed up by that Lion Smoke dog, who may have had a point, I thought.

I fed all of the other dogs while Sam fed just Martha. For all she's so geared up and birdy, she's a motherly type and knew Sam well enough by now to be very concerned, winding herself around him in a vain attempt to make her body a shelter for his, as she would one day do for her pups. She licked his hand in meticulous detail, and Sam stayed for it, and his face too.

Then there was a last hosing and squeegeeing of the runs for the day. When we were done with that, Sam said, "I'm sorry." I waited as Sam looked at me full in the face, with the early-evening light acting like a chisel on the best marble, defining the clear edges of his features against the mountains behind the kennel.

"Love. Somehow. Love. I mean, women, that's what I mean, or the goddamn inconvenience."

"Sex?"

"Yes. No, I mean love. It doesn't fit my life. No one, nobody *fits*, except you. You're the only one I know that I really know who you are. I'm sorry, but I hated Luke coming here, could have torn him up sometimes, which is ridiculous, because he's got guts and a real mind, and maybe he knows who you are, and it's not as though I ever . . . ah, hell."

"Guts?" I had thought this about Luke, too, when he wasn't doing his protective mother-preacher act, and I had thought it because it was true, but I didn't know what to say.

"You remember, just before Lion tore you, the way he laughed when you were cross about him letting Prince mouth off while he worked—that is something we don't do much of, largely because we usually aren't working our own dogs or for long, but Luke did that. Was it without malice and still respect-fully? I hope it's enough for you, Annie, he's going to do that. But I don't know how you did it."

"How I did what?"

"Fell in love with Luke that way, so that he could be here."

Now that was one I had some sort of answer to, and an answer Sam would not only accept, but understand. The answer went something like: Because I have seen who he is. But that was not quite what Sam meant; Sam knew all of love's ways of knowing. What Sam meant and couldn't say because he couldn't find a justification for saying it and wouldn't without one, now that he was calmer, was: *Why* is he hanging around the kennel so goddamn much?

So I said, "Well, he fits pretty well. Most of the time he fits." I hoped it was true. My skin said it was, most of the time.

"I—yeah, okay, I can see that. If you think so. . . . You've got to have what you want, Annie." Sam hit his fist absently against the concrete-block wall of the grooming room.

Ten
HANDS
ON AT
LAST

After that I felt a bit . . . stale, somehow, and Luke wasn't fitting in so well now, after Lion's bite, and I accused him about half a dozen times in that many days of not understanding anything he ought to have learned from working Prince, and he started trotting out arguments that were so much like the Burton admirer's that I found that I could not listen for minutes at a time and didn't need to. I could tune back in for a few seconds and know exactly where we were in the script, and Luke could, too, but we weren't talking about anything we wanted to talk about. I soon found that Sam had really broken up with Jenny this time. He and Jenny used to do this regularly, but something in Sam's heart had lurched away from her in a final way, and maybe something shifted for her, too, and I couldn't talk about that with Luke, who couldn't talk to me about much of anything

96

and who had taken to staying the night every so often back up in Oak Glen. He said he wanted to sell the place and had to work on it.

That is roughly how things were when Jouster found us, or rather, answered our summons.

One morning soon after the Lion episode—my arm was still pretty sore and my heart, too—Jerry Slough called to say that the dog he had shown me had bitten Mrs. Skeffington and had a habit of lunging incontinently for anyone in sight when the mood took him, so did we still need a White German Shepherd?

Sam said, "We didn't have to look anymore at all!" He grinned, saying. "We've got the dog, we didn't have to do anything!" And maybe Sam was right. He *was* right, but it does seem to keep turning out that you can't find the right dog unless you keep looking even when you've found him, and why should this be an exception, even though it plainly was?

We agreed to take the dog and to pay Jerry instead of trying to go through the Skeffingtons; one thing I trust Jerry on implicitly is which customers you have as little direct dealings with as possible. I was just a little uneasy about the descriptions of the dog's behavior, but he had enough presence, so I could get from him at least a credible performance of nobility, which was enough of a prospect for me. It was late and I would have to press the dog, and he might get nasty about that, but it was the performance that mattered most, the painting I could never do, but I could at least agree to be a prop-department aide for someone who, I hoped, could.

Slough was called from the road and said he couldn't pick up the dog until Thursday—this was Monday—so Sam and I insisted that we would go right away to the wrecking yard and pick up the dog and give Jerry a postdated check. A check for $475, I should say, which was either way too little or else way too much, and Jerry Slough knew damn well that he couldn't sell that dog to anyone else now that he had a reputation; Mrs. Skeffington seemed to have been thrilled by her nip and her narrow escape from a savage dog and told all of her customers about it. However, Jerry also knew, and we knew, that it was probably that dog or none for us at this point.

Mrs. Skeffington was at her post behind the desk in the front part of the shop when we came by. Women showed up in our classes with extraordinary colors of hair, but I thought no one dyed their hair pink anymore, surely not to match a pantsuit.

I ought to have felt some sympathy for her, I suppose, for she obviously spent a lot of time trying to find an outer frame for confidence, but dog trainers think first about work and then safety, and worry about being virtuous if there is any time left over, or they try to worry about virtue, and all the cards weren't in on Jouster; he *could* turn out to be the sort of dog who would have been fine if he hadn't lived with people like the Skeffingtons and learned hatred thereby. So there wasn't any time left over.

She rang a buzzer we could hear sounding in the back, to summon her husband. Sam and I idled around, examining the bits and pieces of car for sale; I even contemplated a tape deck for my Toyota, but the car is so small, I need all the room I can get for equipment, and even so I have to tie things on the roof or use the dog trailer.

Skeffington appeared in a few minutes with a dog on a leash, a chain leash. I said a dog, but this was The Dog, of course, Jouster. He glanced at me, then past me down the long counter, piled with auto parts and key-ring displays, toward Sam.

Then he lunged for Sam. The chain leash tore up Skeffington's hands, and he let go with a howl of pain—no one can hold on to those goddamn chain leashes if a dog like that decides he has somewhere to go. There was vengeance almighty in that dog, but his sense of strategy was as yet undeveloped, so he charged past me to get to Sam. There was a handy-sized length of radiator hose on the counter, so I grabbed it up and then came down with it, *hard,* on his nose.

The dog stopped, made himself lower while he shook his head in pained puzzlement, spent a second or two working out my intentions, got it right about me, shook his whole self and then settled into as gentlemanly a posture as you please, his tongue lolling politely, like one who says, "Oh. Well, why didn't you say so? Nobody said anything to me about it!"

Sam and I looked at each other and kept down, just barely, the laughter of surmise, so that's what kind of incurably ferocious man-eating dog he was. No biter he, I sang to myself. It just hadn't occurred to anyone to say, "Don't bite!" What people say instead, to dogs like Jouster and other dogs, is, 'Oooohhhh, that's not nice," and "How could you do that!" or "Don't you want to be a good dog?" or "This sort of behavior is going to ruin your reputation."

I mean that all I said was, "Stop that!"

What he said was, "Okay. Now what?" Sam and I didn't dare laugh, but he was something else; there was even humor in the dog.

I will not try to tell you about the pastel regrets that oozed from the Skeffingtons once they saw the dog transformed and under control. The regrets weren't for the dog, just those momentary regrets some of us feel in the presence of what we suddenly think we could have done—I feel this about Jane Goodall, for example, or I did once, before we had the kennel, felt, *There is a magnificence, a knowledge, that will never be mine,* and I am not especially interested in chimpanzees or life at Gombe. So I knew what their weakness was. It was the dog's magnificence that made up their regrets. That is not what magnificence is for, but sometimes any magnificence will do that, when a human being is feeling too, too human, fragile, capable of dying, and the reason for the kennel was that that is not what magnificence is for.

We got home. I took Jouster out—the Skeffingtons had said that was his name, had been when they got him—intending to try him for about fifteen minutes. I was as unable to come back in sensibly as if I were a twelve-year-old boy in a story about a great field-trial dog or something. Sam came back out and watched for a while, but today even his presence was distracting, because I was afraid Sam could see. . . .

Of course Sam could see. I was afraid of Jouster, not in particular, but along with the rest of the dogs in the world except for Homer. Dogs had become hard to read, less visible. Ever since the bite from Lion. My classes had been getting anxious, because I was so hesitant about which dogs I used for demonstrations. The same thing had happened to Sam after Vietnam, too many corpses, and I had stayed on top of him, had him stay with it—a loss of nerve that was merely a physical reaction; you wait it out the way you wait out any other pain. Later I could be able to say to Sam. "Well, I stuck to the medium-sized dogs. The big ones can do too much damage, and the little ones are nasty!" and Sam would laugh with me, but I could never say that to Luke, because I hadn't been with Luke through the kind of troubles I'd seen Sam through, and because I had lost more than my nerve, had given some reality to Luke that I should have kept, hadn't known I could lose. If I said it to Luke, everything would be in question. There I was with The Dog, afraid that my moment of clear action and vision at Skeffington's Auto Parts was an interlude in what now would be a tentative life.

Consequently I grabbed to get reality back by working Jouster for close to three hours, which no twelve-year-old boy of the sort I have in mind would do, at top speed most of that time, with two- to three-minute breaks here and there. If he hadn't been Jouster, he would have given up in rage or exhaustion twenty times that afternoon. And my fear made me unable to judge the moment to give him a break, which is about as basic as not knowing the difference between a Pekingese and a Newfoundland.

Jouster would snap at me over the next weeks, but that

wasn't what made me afraid. I put pretty hard pressure on him, and he was the kind of dog that knows what he deserves and has the gumption to draw boundaries even after he knows how decisively you can draw your own boundaries with him. I would tell all of this to Homer in the evenings, wishing I could tell it to Luke, afraid that he would appropriate my fear, which was just a physical accident, and make it into a judgment. But I am getting ahead of that day.

Sam said nothing. Sam doesn't go spilling his heart knowledge in vain, and to say anything would have been to give the fear a welcome, so Sam said nothing, just watched off and on until I put the dog up. Put him up with only a feeble version of the anticipation of camaraderie that usually comes from beginning with dogs, especially mighty-hearted ones.

When I came back from the runs and put the collar and long line on the equipment board, Sam was sitting with a calendar in front of him on his working table. He let me know the news.

"You might," he said slowly, addressing his hands, which were on his knees, "might have to put in quite a few such sessions if we're going to make it."

I was too hot and tired to do anything but stand there with my hands hanging. My arm throbbed from the work.

"I called Kaye. Said we had the dog. I think he was drunk, but he didn't sound *too* drunk. 'Great,' he said. 'Bring him on in and let's have a look.' Okay. We hang up.

"Then Kaye called back, not five minutes later. He wasn't bluffing, after all, it seems. They're supposed to start shooting in six weeks. On location. The director is not one to stick to a script, so you have to work him for all sorts of eventualities." He stopped and looked at me. "What did I say, Di? Guess what I said."

I was so tired, I had to think about this, but then I said, "Only one thing you could have said, because you are a goddamn fool dog trainer and don't know any better than to say it. Our business may collapse if you can't hold it together while I work Jouster. We may both go nuts. They probably won't start shooting in six weeks, so we're risking all of this for what may still be a wisp of dream, Jouster or no Jouster. What you did was, you said we'd be there and ready. You don't know any better and you never will, and neither will I."

How deep was the happiness of knowing Sam, I thought, adding, "The only thing in this that might make it work is that I don't think Jouster knows any better, either."

Sam said, "Nope. Dog doesn't know any better. Here's his chance to fill out his name, and he's going to do it too. If you and I do."

If you work animals for Hollywood much at all, you get used to requests for miracles, but I was figuring on a couple of months lead time to get Jouster doing the routines, and that was pushing it from the category of real training into the category of tricks. Six months and more of straight work is a respectably speedy effort if you want some reliable scent work on the dog in addition to the rest of it, and if you also plan to use the dog as a man-trailer at some point. In front of a camera, sending a dog to retrieve something tiny—a toothpick, say—by scent enables you to get through a lot of scenes, from dog-rushes-to-window-to-watch-anxiously-as-criminals-approach to heartwarming reunion scene or, as in *It's A Dog's Life*, to get the dog pacing back and forth, uncannily looking like the father-to-be he is playing.

I was going to have to put more pressure on Jouster than I had ever put on any dog. He was almost bound to collapse or explode in that kind of pressure-cooker situation, especially if I continued to be afraid of dogs.

Of course, I thought this over and said, "No particular problem." Sam let the anxious irony slide off into the breeze coming through the window.

This was a big promise I was making, in the casual tones of

a promise you can't help but keep. It meant that if Luke pressed me for a choice between him and Jouster's work, I would work Jouster, which was what I was doing, anyway, but not, as it were, officially, because Luke hadn't said anything.

Sam looked at me for a moment, doing his sentient granite pose, and I could practically have given you a photograph of what was going on behind his forehead, behind those calm eyebrows. Sam's a lot like Homer. He knew as well as I did what this meant, how it would have to go.

■

Which is how it went. Sam took over just about all of my kennel duties, including my classes, which lost us some students, because two classes had to be canceled.

He took Lion Smoke over altogether, too, right in the middle of making some headway with the both of us working with her—not that there's much to choose between Sam and me when we have a leash in our hands, but now we had started taking her into parks and downtown, and it helped to have someone to distract her if a passerby got too intimate. Not that there was a problem anymore. Sam had won with Lion, and the big, burly dog's choleric responses turned out to be just accidents of her personal history; and the Airedale gaiety and choreography became dominant. The hound in her showed now only as a seriousness about trailing that was unterrierlike, and in a bit more heaviness of build and movement than you get in an Airedale. She was staunch beside Sam now, straight on her legs and encompassing in the eyes, and her coat had had time to come back so that the dark steel-gray of her saddle and the dense mahogany of her furnishings could have been a standard for the standard. She stood a bit taller than Jouster, but so compactly built that when she was with Sam, he simply looked a bit shorter.

Our commitment to the movie meant neither of us getting

a second off except for sleep, or really including sleeping time—
if you want to train dogs, you have to have the right dreams.
Also, if you want to work out human-to-human love, you have
to have the right dreams. Besides all that, I was not going to be
able to do much with Homer, until it looked as though I could
do things with both him and Jouster, for a while. The Wolfhound would survive the neglect, but that sort of thing nags
away at the heart. There was no chance Homer's heart would be
rubbed away, but there might be some sore spots for a while.

In my chest there was a throb, a hope that Luke would stay
through whatever was coming. Everything that went into my
decision had only taken six hours to happen in, from Slough's
call to Sam's, and Luke wasn't around for any of it. He had gone
up into the high desert to the Willie Boy monument, Willie Boy,
a Chemuevi Indian, had been the object of a famous manhunt
in 1909 in this area, and there is a book about him. He ran off
with his girlfriend to get away from her pa; maybe he killed her
pa. There was a movie. Anyway, floods a year or so back had
washed out the road to the monument, so you couldn't get there
by car anymore; maybe with a dune buggy or a heavy-duty jeep
you could, or a mule or a horse or maybe even a donkey.

Luke had found out about the monument and the manhunt, had been over to Riverside, to the Mission Inn, which had
been a center of activities while the hunt was going on, because
of a vist from President Taft. He was going to write about it, but
before he did, he wanted to go there himself on horseback so
his article could include sufficient warning of the dangers of
getting stuck or lost, but mainly I think just because he wanted
a reason to ride and camp out. He had planned to be gone from
three to six days; the day we bought Jouster was the fifth day he
had been gone.

He got back late that night. By the time he arrived, Jouster
was doing exercises that belonged in the third and fourth weeks,
not the seventh and eighth hours, of work. He was heeling and

sitting as noble as Rin-Tin-Tin in a true-to-life story, doing sit-stays and down-stays, too, and working on the stand as well as beginning retrieving and jumping. I had the schedule worked out like this: I would work Jouster for around fifteen or twenty minutes, sleep for twenty minutes, and so on. Any corners were cut into sleeping, not training time. In a day or two I hoped to be able to sleep an hour, or at least forty-five minutes, at a time, but not now. This was twenty-four hours a day.

Luke was full of anecdotes from his trip, but I wasn't able to listen to them, nor was I able to tell him why not in any detail. I did toss him a beer when he came in, on my way out to the training area, to turn on the lights for another session. Jouster was a bit tired but still game—he grumbled at me a bit on the down but that was all. I was leaving Jouster in the run, so that he would not be distracted from thinking over what was going on.

On my way out I had said to Luke that I wanted to show him something. He may not have heard, but he followed me and drew in his breath as Jouster appeared, looking as if he were coated in spun pearls in the moonlight.

Luke stopped for a moment, stiller than a tree waiting for the sun to rise. Then he practically came to attention, gave a whoop like a TV cowboy, and said, "That is him, isn't it? That's the dog, the one Slough brought by that night?"

"Yeah," I said vaguely, surprised that Luke recognized the dog.

"So I'm really off the hook. I haven't stopped your movie."

"Huh?" Then I said, "Hey, It *can't* be your fault. Things around a kennel always turn out to be a dog trainer's fault. It goes with the territory. I am the dog trainer here, the only one now that Sam has gone to sleep for the night." I was too tired, too full of thoughts about Jouster's work to go on, but it was true that everything was the trainer's fault. Or responsibility.

Luke said, "Right. You're a dog trainer. Just don't forget it." As he was grinning, he made a move—to hug me, perhaps—

and Jouster, all watchdog, alerted on him. No growling, snarling, no breaking his position, but alerting on Luke nonetheless. Luke tensed, started to speak and stopped.

In that tensing of the ears, that evocation by the dog of the dog within the dog, he did what twelve months of lectures couldn't do by way of telling anyone what a working dog is. Since Jouster didn't know Luke from Adam (and me not much better), that was the correct move, the right decision, but it bothered Luke and I knew why. It is humiliating to be stopped in your tracks by what someone might swear was the mere ear twitch of a dog, and the thought passed through my mind that it was humiliation that made the Skeffingtons want the dog out of their shop. Especially when what you had been expecting was welcome.

Luke, whose fatigue I suddenly saw, even in the moonlight, relaxed and said amiably enough. "Well, when you get around to it, you might tip him off about my being in residence here." He failed to make this sound like a mere good-natured bit of ribbing, and it came over me that I could probably spare half an hour to hear about his trip, and more than that, that I wanted to hear, but I didn't think this in time to say anything, just kept myself there by Jouster, not yet giving him the release command.

I realized that what Luke had said was true. He did live there. I had to table that thought for later consideration, probably after the shooting of the film was over.

"What's his name?" Luke asked.

"Same as it's always been, I guess. Someone somewhere named him Jouster." Jouster's ears flicked in affirmation.

"Just Jouster?"

I released Jouster and went to sit with Luke. It meant talk instead of sleep, just this once. Jouster looked me over in this unfamiliar capacity, looked Luke all over, made the right assessment of the situation and lay down in front of us, as if he had read about some hearth creature in Dickens, or in Kipling's story in which the dog is First Friend.

"Well, that's his name. You can see that it is."

"Okay. But don't you want something fancier for the books?"

"There aren't any books. The dog's got no papers. What you see, and what the vet sees, that's all you get, just this dog and his name."

"Jouster . . . justice . . . jester . . . How about Diane's Jesting Prince Jouster?" It came out even sappier when he said it than it looks here on the page.

I giggled. "Yeah, and several thousand dollars worth of film and crew time go by before I finish even saying his name, much less getting around to working him in a scene. Remember, Jouster doesn't have to pay Social Security or answer to the IRS. Just me. Jouster answers just to me when I say his name."

I was a little high on the glory of it all, and it got into my voice, so Jouster got up smoothly and placed himself—not pushing, mind you—between my legs and Luke's as we sat there. I thought, exultant, "He's mine! Jouster's my dog! He's *my* dog!" This is a Shepherd thing, other breeds do it, but Shepherds are the clearest about it, interposing themselves that way, possessive, protective, bold. Jouster was genuinely mine, after only half a day. It can happen like that.

I babbled a little more to Luke about Jouster, then asked him about his trip. He said he had gotten a little copy for the paper, and a lot of thinking out of it.

"Thinking about what?"

"Oh, about . . . writing. Me and writing."

His eyes were strong and full of light as he said this, and I wanted to hear more, but it was time to go out and work Jouster again. I did, with Luke watching.

After the work, Jouster and Homer made their agreement. Jouster rested, then approached Homer, who rose, knowing that this *was* a moment, that Jouster wasn't just another client's dog, and they made a gallantry together. Jouster turned with his hind end in place, saying his magnificence of agility; being smaller than Homer, he could turn better close, and he showed all of this, and Homer followed it in grave arcs, and then Homer angled over Jouster as he took Jouster and about twenty feet of ground in one ease, one stride, and Jouster stood, accepting this in his turn, and then the two dogs made their partnership, working out a schedule of the evening patrol of the kennel, Jouster taking the closer turns, Homer taking the arcs. They were both Alpha males, and Homer would not forget, if Jouster broke any rules of chivalry, who had seniority, any more than Jouster would forget that seniority isn't everything, but they made their quest of each other and returned. Jouster stayed just behind Homer's shoulder, until they were close to me, and then he moved forward, to mark for me his awareness of our new friendship. Homer stayed close but didn't interfere.

Jouster's tail moved lightly, a flag of good fellowship and courtesy but also ready to make anyone who was discourteous in his view answer to Jouster. Ready for the consequences of his decisions and any of mine, and that such a dog should have arrived in Slough's hands and then the Skeffingtons' made you believe there was such a thing as justice, because his past history seemed like a crime against Justice taking the form for the moment of Jouster.

Jouster's justice was tempered, good-humored justice, on this evening. He leaned against my leg for assurance, and I wasn't afraid of dogs. It was again time for sleep, but Luke had been gone five days, so we went back into the cottage to talk some more, with an honor guard that now included Prince, who had been left in the car when Luke first drove home, when Jouster was still an unknown quantity to Luke. We were back in the living room.

Luke said, watching Jouster, "Well, I heard Sam talking about background, how even without the papers you can see background in a dog. I was thinking of the Kelpies we had on the ranch. They were just rough-and-tumble ranch dogs, cattle dogs, but they would go into anything for Esther or her fore-man, get a cow or a steer to behave, discourage wolves, even a bear once, stay in the hot sun until their jobs were finished. He, Esther's foreman, always said that a good animal can have the wrong name but never too many names, so I thought about adding something to honor his background; even if we don't know it. How about, oh, how about Nimble Jouster, Prince of . . . something."

"Everybody wants to call German Shepherds Prince or Duke or King or something. A Jouster is what he is. That's the only name he needs."

Luke continued to look at Jouster. For some reason the steady, direct eye contact with a comparative stranger didn't bother Jouster, though it would most dogs and most people. Luke has this way of holding you in those clear gray eyes once in a while. If Luke weren't messed up by having the usual sad history of human beings, he would be like Homer, I thought.

I offered weakly, "Swift Joust and Fire Dance?"

Luke said thoughtfully, "He was her groom, wasn't he?"

"Groom? Who got married?"

"Oh, an old story about Justice. Says she just got disgusted and fled, leaving the world to fend for itself without her, but she admired one or two humans and took pity on them all, so she sent her groom back, to . . ."

It was late now, and I was surprised to realize Sam had walked into the room, in fact had been there for some time, registering on some periphery of awareness for me. For a change from what had become his usual demeanor lately, he didn't look so closed up, nor sound it as he said, "Dog's coming along all right."

Which means, by the way, in Sam's way of talking, that the dog is a miracle and the training I'm doing is a mega-miracle, a gift from the angels. That's how Sam says that sort of thing, or else he says, "Not too shabby." That's one of the things I like about Sam. No hype, which didn't mean he couldn't talk when he wanted to.

Then Sam said, "I'm making more coffee. Any takers?" On his way out of the room, he turned slightly without stopping and said, astonishing Luke and even startling me a little—Sam didn't often talk about the books he used to inhabit—"Astrea. My father read it to me—in Spenser the name of justice is Astrea.

"She got fed up with the world because it kept looking like 'Nam, and left, and now she's the constellation Virgo, but because there was a Knight of Justice, a kind of incorruptible cop, she took pity and she set her squire to help him. The squire was called . . ."

I said, "Talus." Sam had told me about Talus once, back when we were first setting up the kennel. Justice really meant something to Sam. When he first told me about Artegal and Talus and his father telling him about it, he said that when he was a kid, he had figured that poetry was a fairy tale, a never-never land, because it had justice in it and the world didn't. So I had said that dog training was the same kind of never-never land in that case, and that's why our kennel is called Neverland Kennel.

Sam said slowly, "Yeah, Talus. The way Spenser has it, Talus is like a dog, iron jaws, iron paws, and Talus wouldn't be a bad name for this dog, but since it's not Talus, how about calling him Jouster, Squire of Justice?"

I felt a frisson of supersititious worry, because that did half seem like the right name, but I wasn't Sam and I sometimes thought I had had enough of justice and her friends in my work with the sheriff's posse. Homer had seen a lot of it, too, my dogs got to see justice, whose landscape had a tendency to have corpses in it. You can get tired of that, and you can want to do a movie instead.

The posse—I should tell you about the posse—did mostly search-and-rescue in the desert, but Dave Buckman, the posse sheriff, had talked me into criminal work too. He had been working to get a police-dog program for the town since before Sam and I opened the kennel, and every time one of my dogs made a bloodless capture or saved a cop, it helped him, and so I used my dogs to help Dave. But Jouster was not for Justice, I hoped. He was the wrong color for police work, anyway, too visible for scouting. But the big thing was, he was for the movie. He was just, but I didn't get him *for* justice. He was going to show something.

Sam noted my uneasiness thoughtfully. "But the old story leaves out the important part about Jouster's name, the one he already has. Like the knights themselves, not the grooms. Jousting and jesting. How about Heaven's Jouster?"

Jouster looked right at Sam, his mouth shut as he mulled it over, and mulled Sam over, looking a bit the way Sam himself does when something registers on him as right. It was right, because with dogs, of course, everything goes all to hell if you go to *choosing* between the jester's court and the magistrate's, like King Lear. Maybe what Jouster liked was that if you put heaven first, you aren't allowed to make really dumb mistakes, but it could also mean that even just slightly wrong moves could be really dumb mistakes. That was right for art, as well as justice, but it's hard to get laughter into justice. Except in heaven, maybe.

You also get to remember, more often than is good for ordinary domestic life, about that part of the dog, the dog that fires the dog, the one God put here that no one gets to take credit for, not even credit for having a good eye for a dog.

Luke said that yes, that was the name. So did I, but I added that it could be his name only as long as we didn't write it down anywhere, which none of us would have thought to do, anyway. When people write down words like *heaven*, they start to get a fix on them. Words like *God* too. There's God, of course, or where did Jouster come from, especially where did he come from already answering to Jouster, even if Slough probably got the name wrong when he picked the dog up, but all the light we need to see by is in front of us, in the direction of a dog's gaze, except at night.

Luke said, "Yes, yes. Not written, not tattooed, not on a registration blank, not on a contract, not in brass letters on a collar, not on the wall. But we can say it."

He went out to the kitchen for some champagne left over from some dog show celebration, and Sam opened the bottle. This got some of the tension between us all out in the open, where it could evaporate and air out a little. Luke started his bit about how Mrs. Skeffington's judgment of the dog had been right, that she didn't deserve to be bitten just because she was annoying. He asked if police dogs standardly bite people for being stupidly scared. I think he meant to tease me, but there was too much at stake, too much knowledge that had to be kept steady, for nonsense to get uttered. It was like this: What Luke said didn't have anything to do with Jouster or with police dogs of any worth, but it was like a rumor, impossible to correct, so the only thing to do was to say another rumor against it. It wasn't Luke's fault, it wasn't his rumor, and he deserved an answer, but I had to work the dog, and I had to get some sleep if I was going to keep it up.

I looked at Sam, who had heard similar nonsense bring down good dogs and good programs, and I thought about Dave's work, and there was nothing wrong with Luke, but I couldn't let his remarks go by.

"The good ones do!" I said. "The good ones know when a bite is in order." Luke said that maybe I sometimes got sentimental about dogs, ever so gently, softening it by saying that everyone tended to get too involved in their work.

Sam said, "Sentimentality makes airbrush drawings of dogs for greeting cards. Annie *works* them."

Luke said, "All right, I see that. But I want to understand."

I said, "I'll explain, Luke. You can come with me on the posse sometime."

That's what I said instead of explaining, and went back out to work Jouster again, Luke and Sam following, holding and pouring champagne, the Event of Jouster's actuality and presence dissolving all of our personal histories. They drank their respect of Jouster—Sam more accurate and casual than Luke, but Luke for all of that correct—while the white dog worked, scattering the dust of Jurupa high into the wind on the moon.

Eleven
JEST AND
NO
JUDGMENT
AND NO
HOMER

It was in the middle of a conversation with Luke about Jouster that I noticed that Sam now had a dog of his own, and that of all dogs, it was Lion, who had done such a thorough number on me. She still didn't belong to Sam legally, of course.

She had started out looking near worthless, with a ragged battle flag of a brain, and now her integrity and the intelligence of her loyalty to Sam glinted off her with every move she made. Lion was Sam's dog, and Sam was Lion's master. Such things happen, but a pro like Sam wouldn't normally have let it happen to him, at least not with someone else's dog.

Sam said, "I think it was the only way she would have gotten trained, Annie. There isn't anyone but me for her—training her was like *remembering* her."

Sam even had taken to having Lion sleep with him in his cottage. This was as involved as he'd ever gotten with a dog, barring Zeus, since I'd met him, but Sam had reasons. With him doing double-time work at the kennel and me doing nothing but eating and sleeping and working Jouster, there was too much to do in the way of handling, setting up equipment, decisions about diet and so on. Which meant that the only way for Sam to do a proper job on Lion was to have her with him virtually twenty-four hours a day, stay on top of her even while he was asleep, because Sam knows what a dog is thinking, whether or not Sam is technically asleep. If Lion were to indulge a stray thought or dream about undeserved bites, Sam got onto her.

So in the circumstances, that had been the only way to handle that dog, but that didn't account for what else was going on.

I did occasional short rounds with Homer, whom I otherwise neglected and left to his own devices. Since he was not a dog to indulge resentment with criminal behavior, his only option was to sit around being resigned, which is what he did. He didn't sulk because he *wouldn't* sulk, and his restraint in the face of Jouster's eating up most of my attention made me feel more aware of him than a hundred dogs of a lesser sort might have made me, however reasonably they pleaded their cases.

I worked Homer, the few times I did, with Jouster ten feet away (on the other side of the fence to the runs, of course), and it was a good bit of education for Jouster, too—the clear lesson being that he was going to have to continue to adjust some of his personal-property theories. He and Jouster had worked out their arrangement already, of course, but Jouster especially needed time to mull over the details. Homer, who had already had numerous lessons of this sort simply by being my dog and going with me while I worked other dogs, didn't need the lesson. Still, there were some tussles between the two of them when they both had to get thumped instead of happily thumping each other. Jouster worked it out readily enough—he had more poise about other dogs, at least about Homer, than I thought he would—but I figured that only if those two dogs ever came to work together on a problem, with two handlers, one for each of them, would the friendship be stabilized. Not that they were going to hurt each other, but Jouster's exclusionary passions would mean that they would have to renegotiate their agreement from time to time. Subtly, of course; a stranger watching them on their rounds would see only working love and be right, at that.

I had been working Jouster on scent discrimination, sending him out to choose the one article out of a group that had the scent he was supposed to find. The life of command between dog and handler expands at this point to include scent, and that's a more intimate matter for a dog, not something a dog is going to hand over to you just like that. It is a kind of testing under fire, at least under blank gunfire, and you just have to hold your breath and pray you don't screw up.

The point of putting formal scent work on Jouster was that it would come in handy on the movie if the director knew anything about dogs. Or even if the director didn't. The director might suddenly want a sentimental and passionate greeting, for example, between an actor and the dog. If the dog has worked scent and you put in the actor's clothes the scent of something the dog loves, the dog will greet the actor like a beloved spouse returned from Hades. Or you can use scent to direct a dog's head movements—let him know that the thing you are sending him for is going to be just outside a window, and if the camera crew and director are on the ball, you'll get a nice shot of an eager Rin-Tin-Tin listening for the return of the stagecoach. There are other, clumsier ways to get such shots, but the results are mechanical-looking.

Jouster, thank heavens, loved formal scent work—which may or may not have anything to do with eventual work on a trail—and was even able to learn formal tracking of human scent at the same time. And he never needed a correction. This scared me because I had no way of testing him against a situation he didn't want to work in—and being motivated by my scent or Sam's or Luke's is not at all the same as being motivated by game or by real man-trailing. I could push him on other work, but I didn't dare push him too far too fast with scent, for fear of ruining him. But it is one thing to scent when you are comfortable, and another when camera crews, directors, hot lights and actors are making everything no fun or distracting, and what would a football or basketball or running coach think about taking athletes to the big time who, however talented, had never been tested against pain or stress or simple, cross moods? Jouster looked competent and full of desire, and that was all I knew for sure.

One day Sam and Freddie and Luke and I were all leaning on the fence, giving the dogs and ourselves a breather. Jouster had just finished the roughest track—which wasn't very rough, a hundred yards with one turn—I dared try on him. I was saying, "I never saw such a thing. It's weird, spooky!"

Sam just nodded his head a millimeter, knowing what I meant. Freddie was silent. Luke, next to Sam with Lion at ease between them, asked, "What's so weird? I must have seen a hundred dogs by now in your classes, and more at dog shows, doing scent work."

I was vaguely impatient with Luke these days, just because I was impatient with anything that wasn't training progress for Jouster. I told him sharply that scent was a queer thing, however you thought it through, talent for it being only incidentally in the nose and largely in the unguessable extent of the dog's desire to track. I said, "And so I can't know until it's perhaps too late whether or not the dog will come through for me."

Luke read this as discouragement and said, "Diane, Jouster's magnificent! He hasn't made a liar out of you yet, and he won't." But Luke didn't know—that was all right, maybe—but he didn't know what he didn't know, and I was becoming more and more aware that there were laws, like natural laws, to the kennel, but not quite natural laws because they could be broken—inside of me. Luke didn't break them—they weren't in him to break. But they were in me.

It was at just that moment that I noticed about Lion and Sam. Sam had called her to heel, and it was in the way he did it and she responded that I saw. Blockheaded as usual, I said so. "Sam! She's your dog now? Owners defaulted on the training bill?"

Sam looked as ordinary and uneventful as he could and said casually, "Nope. But they're still afraid of her."

"But," I said—and this was also the first time I'd noticed it—"but you've got her now about as reliable as a dog ever gets! A little longer and she could earn her kibble baby-sitting around the neighborhood."

"Hell, she was always like that, just nobody really believed it." That was Sam; Sam believed in belief. "At this point," he would say to his classes, "your dog will probably do exactly what you imagine he's going to do. So imagine that he obeys." Sam had imagined the Dog inside the varmint Lion had been. I had to keep imagining the Dog inside the dog, in Jouster.

"But the owners are still afraid of her?" I said this hopefully.

"Well, it's possible I'll have to talk to them again."

Luke, hearing this exchange, bent down and picked up Martha, the little English Cocker Sam had been working and did an elegant little dance with her out of sheer gaiety, whirling her around while Prince came up on his hind legs and did his best to cha-cha-cha.

Then I saw that Sam and Luke had, as males sometimes can without a word said that I know of, walked out of their small Cold War, for the moment at least, and into the more delicate and sometimes dangerous heat of love and friendship. And saw that Jouster had seen it all, too, and without so much as moving any muscle named in your anatomy texts. Jouster watched Luke more tenderly now, but he watched him. It's this about dogs, especially a good Shepherd, that they know what we don't about how our places are put together, they note everything that belongs and doesn't, and so even though it was Jouster who was the newcomer, he knew that Luke wasn't in the kennel the way Sam and Freddie and I were. When I saw this, it made my skin too tight, and I would see it and put it away again, it was too much to know. I put it away by saying to myself, Maybe Jouster is just too suspicious. He should accept Luke, Luke was in residence here when he arrived. But that was wrong. Jouster wasn't suspicious, he was just registering.

While I continued training Jouster, Luke spent a fair amount of time away from the kennel, sometimes at the library, I suppose, but once I saw him in Denney's, writing, writing, writing. That time I had been on my way with Jouster to the feed and tack store for a lesson on not molesting chicks, ducklings and baby rabbits or the tack-store owner's tabby cat and lovebirds, and I didn't think anything except that one of Luke's feature stories must be lengthening into a book. I remembered his cry that he had wanted to be a novelist, and of course I had heard about Tolstoy starting to write fiction when he was even older than Luke was, but I didn't think about it then. Everybody I knew had wanted to be a novelist or painter or something, but people don't, in one's own real life, become novelists just like that. Luke was in my bed at night, warm and welcoming, and in bed I felt, saw and heard nothing else but Luke there, with Homer and Jouster on the floor.

The day after Luke's dance with Martha, Jouster followed me out to work a track in a pasture full of thorns, stickers, burrs and at least twenty of the kinds of weed California is famous for among veterinarians because they produce irritants and allergens dogs are especially susceptible to. They call it the California disease. There were weeds so odorous *I* could smell them, and cowpats too. Jouster streamlined his way through as if it were a pristine meadow of clean, new grass and delicate scents, including the one he was after, instead of the scent equivalent of Grand Central Station. That was the day we started actual tracking—meaning on a track I didn't know—and by the end of that day I knew what I had, or at least I knew more than I'd dared so much as guess at before.

Equipment stored away that evening, Jouster and I went looking for Luke. He was in Sam's kitchen, and I opened with, "Luke! Sam! Knock on wood, but this just may be a for-real cold-trailing hound I got here!"

Sam lifted his eyebrows, which in Sam means pleasure, curiosity, encouragement. Luke asked for an account. But Homer . . . Jouster was wearing Homer's harness, which I had fitted up and made myself, just for Homer. There wasn't time to make a separate harness for Jouster, and Homer's was the only one we had that was about the right size for him. Homer walked over to Jouster and sniffed the harness. I hadn't taken Homer into that pasture for a while, partly because you don't want tracking to become noxious to a dog, and also because you had to schedule half an hour or so to get all the burrs and foxtails and so on out of the dog's coat and paws afterward. There was no reproach in Homer, but Sam took over the task of cleaning Jouster, and Homer and I tracked a little that night. He wasn't full of enthusiasm, but it was a hot, smoggy evening.

The next day, for me and Jouster, was a little retrieving, polishing his reliability on that and then just tracking, tracking, all sorts of tracks. I've never known a dog I felt was driving me to keep working on tracking—it's strenuous, and in our climate the dog's nose gets full of dust and pollen. We tracked Sam and Luke and the neighbor's banty rooster, who made a complicated trail on his way from one of his henhouses to another, newer

one. Toward the end of the day a lady came in to leave her Shih
Tzu for boarding, and I had her lay me a short track, which
Jouster worked, almost as fresh as he had been hours ago when
we'd started the day's work.

Sam contrived to be near us as much as possible while he
worked his dogs, and I got to look up from my work sometimes
and find Sam there, looking like a partner, saying things such
as, "That's going to have to be some movie to live up to this dog.
Not too shabby." Sam and I talked a lot then, in training breaks,
about what a movie would be like that showed what dog training
really was. We knew better, we really did, than to think that
Hollywood was any place to put the soul's money, but we imagined it, anyway.

"We could write our own script," Sam would say. "Take the
story of almost anyone in our classes who puts real open work
on their dog. Show what the dog does. I've got it: Scene one is
Joe Shmoe the day after the first lesson, trying to get the long
line untangled, reading the instruction sheet, totally discon-
nected. In each training scene the lines get less and less tangled,
and then invisible, made of light, a scene where the dog works
down a shaft of sunlight. . . ."

"Yeah. Or a scene where it's Josephine Schmoe, and her dog
is climbing the leash for her throat in scene one, and by the end
they've formed their own little ninja, a kind of Robin Hood-style
ninja. . . ."

"Yeah, set in Israel, and Josephine is an immigrant from
America, and the Israelis think she isn't cutting it very well, and
they rout out a PLO enclave, and even Israeli intelligence doesn't
know about it, and Josephine keeps looking klutzy, as her
disguise, and the dog is an Airedale or a Bouvier, so the dog
can act like a clown. . . ."

"But the dog has to be Jouster," I would add. So I taught
Jouster to clown. He wasn't a trick dog, but by then I figured he
would do anything for me, and in a few days he had a nice little

circus act together. He imitated a Poodle, learned to pounce on imaginary insects, his rear end wagging in the air; he covered his face with his paw and even spun in the air on the command—"Twirl!"—as well as barking on command. I liked the Israeli plot: jesting and justice. Jouster was less jest than justice, but he did the clowning fine, anyway.

Again, the evening after Jouster tracked the lady with the Shih Tzu, Sam cleaned and fed Jouster for me, and I worked Homer for a few minutes, then went for a walk with him, since he hadn't much enthusiasm for work and I didn't have the time to work out how to raise his energy and desire.

One time, Jouster and I came in from working, I plopped down on a kitchen chair as usual, inhaling iced tea and wiping the sweat and grit off my face. Jouster tanked up on water and then, instead of flaking out like a normal dog would after work that hard, he sat beside me until I asked, not with my voice, what was he ready to do now? And then I would know what it was, and we would go do it.

I had been noticing gradually and out of the corner of my eye, as it were, in this period, that Luke had put Prince back on a check line and was stopping him from mouthing off when he ran the relay hurdles, and that Sam had Lion beginning on them, not scenting yet but retrieving over two hurdles, and then three and four, without the scent platform, to help Luke out. This particular evening I complimented Luke on Prince's work, and he said Sam had gotten him interested in getting together a team to challenge Chicago and L.A. that year at Superdog.

He paused before what he obviously thought of as a risky remark and said, "Sam said that no faults are scored against a dog for barking in a relay race." Then he added, "But Sam showed me that it was slowing Prince down, and his time is improving." He smiled his pride in Prince, and his love, and I got a bit wobbly and thought that while I knew the twenty-four-hour-a-day training program wasn't going to last much longer, maybe Luke didn't, and maybe I ought to take a break and spend more time with Luke, but there were the other questions such as, When did I want to do this? What would it cost me and Jouster?

A day later, when I found Homer no longer able to work, the world shifted again. He had stopped eating, though he would try when I asked him to. A gallant dog like that can break your heart trying. But I went on working Jouster every hour, because I thought I had to.

I would talk to Homer, ask him to eat, and the first couple of days he managed to force himself to do it. When he could no longer pretend, he would look up at me and make apologies. Not like a child apologizing but more like a knight of the realm, the sweep of his tail saluting me. I finally had sense enough to leave Jouster in his run and take Homer to the vet. Sam came with me.

This was not old Doc Adams, on whom I had relied since childhood. He was out of commission now with arthritic troubles, so I had to put up with the youngster who had bought the practice. He seemed like no vet at all after old Doc Adams, full of that slickness that you're seeing more and more these days, which wasn't his fault but U.C. Davis', which was trying to turn out vets as phony as M.D.s, as Sam said, and I was pretty pissed off with the cosmos just then (instead of myself), because my dog was sick, so I was sharp with the poor vet when he was admiring Homer in a friendly way.

The vet said, "That's a big, good-looking fellow."

I said half crazy, "Never mind that he's big and beautiful, he's also sick, and you'd better take good care of him." And Sam put his hand on Homer's forearm, in place of putting it on my arm. The vet looked unfinished.

Nonetheless, it seemed right when he said he wanted to hang on to Homer for testing—he was proposing a day or two. I proposed an hour or two and lost. He said it looked like an arthritic hip developing, which was a mistake, but he did find the mouth ulcers I hadn't had the wit to check for.

I followed him back to the kennel where he put Homer in a comfortable run. When I asked Homer to take the step up into the run, he looked around at me, to tell me it would pain him, but he would go ahead and do it if I said so, he was just double-checking with me, and I said so, and he went in.

I wanted to talk to Homer but was stuck with nothing more to say to him except, in what I hoped was the voice I use at the beginning of a new tracking exercise. "Yeah, I know it looks bad, but it is a thing to get beyond. Hang in there." Or some such.

Twelve
JOUSTER
AND THE
POSSE

That was in the late morning; the vet said he'd call in the early evening.

When I got back home, there was a call from Dave Buck-man, the foreman of the sheriff's posse. Chuck Olsen, who owned a local furniture store, had called because his little girl had been kidnapped up in the high desert while they were there for a day's outing in the Joshua Tree Monument, which is a desert wildlife park, one of the most spectacular deserts in the world. He was nearly hysterical but able to remember where he had left the kidnapper, near a curve in the road some way from the family's picnic site.

He and his wife and their little girl, Amy, had gone up to spend the day at the Joshua Tree park. They found they hadn't brought enough soft drinks and food, as people often don't who aren't used to the park. So Mrs. Olsen drove back to town to fetch more. While she was gone, the child disappeared during a walk Olsen took with her. When she returned, to hear her daughter was gone, she must have screamed, but there isn't a scream large enough to fill the high desert, you hear sounds up there all right, but they don't linger; the air is too sharp and thin—from God's breathlessness, some say.

While searching among the rocks that are the size of hills on the mountainside, Olsen encountered a man in a loose white hood with a gun who had the child with him. He forced Olsen to drive him higher up and got out with the child, telling Olsen to drive back to his wife. Olsen would hear from him. He told him it would cost him $100,000 to get her back.

Olsen and his wife rushed back to Jurupa, drove all the way before calling anyone and first called Mrs. Olsen's father, since they didn't have anything like the $100,000, and then Olsen called the police.

Since there weren't likely to be other human trails where the white mask had disappeared, there was some chance the trail was still there, and perhaps a dropped cigarette package or something that would give the police a sense of direction.

With Homer ill, Jouster was the closest we had to a man-trailer of any sort. I had worked him with a view more to filming situations than posse situations, but there was no one else. Jouster was green, and we had nothing to give him a scent of the white mask, but we had a stuffed Raggedy-Ann doll that Mrs. Olsen swore no one but Amy ever touched, and the car would still have the kidnapper's scent if we hurried. It was a strange desert story.

I told Dave that Jouster was unlikely to be ready for this, and Dave said, "Well, it's a kid. Let's give it a go. We have the helicopters going over the area, anyway, but let's give the dog a go at it first."

Dave is a large, even fat man, but he can stay on a job or a trail from dawn to dusk and dusk to dawn in any weather, knows the desert the way I know Homer and keeps his horses fit, teaching them on practice rides with the other men to know the desert his way.

The call about Homer would probably come long before we returned. I told Luke, who said he had to go into L.A., but of course there was Sam to wait for the call, and Freddie for the runs and any calls to Sam's house.

This was the first kidnapping I'd had to deal with, though it wasn't the first time I had been glad I was a dog handler and not a cop. The terrain up there isn't wonderful for ambush, but there are possibilities, and since I would have to be one hundred percent occupied in watching the dog, I had to have backup. Dave and his men were as good as backup gets, which was something of a comfort. The other, more grisly, comfort was that the dog was the one the creeps were likely to go for first if we got that close to them, which gave you and your backup time to get them, maybe—or at least stay alive.

It was also the first time in quite a while I'd had to deal with anything without Zeus or Duke or Homer, who was maybe dying in that blasted vet's office.

When Dave arrived to pick us up, he got out of the car and looked down at Jouster. He had come in a squad car, with two uniformed cops. Officers O'Rourke and Gesner. O'Rourke and Jouster and I rode crowded in the back. We didn't necessarily expect to find the kidnapper. There was no place for him to hole up in Joshua Tree itself, but Jouster, if he worked, could tell us that he wasn't there—or it might be they—or lead us to a spot where the kidnapper's car had been and thus to some information. If we did find the suspect, Dave would call for a car to transport him. Or them.

Olsen, who was driving alone in his own car so as to preserve any scent there might be, met us at the kennel. Apparently he'd been curious about it. He had the kind of fat that comes from greed rather than pleasure, or it feels that way to me. I knew what he'd be like in a training class, and I glanced at Sam, who was having the same vision I suspected. Olsen's dog wouldn't exist for him except for the eyes; the rest would be smoke. The dog would be big, expensive and would have a straight hind end, and Olsen would look around fatly, fantasizing everyone admiring his dog. The dog would be a Great Dane who would forgive him for performing perversions of training that ought to earn him a bite. I didn't even want to shake his hand.

But he was a victim, and while I wasn't sworn to protect him, I was committed to helping Dave, who was. And there was his little girl, who wouldn't necessarily inherit her father's pig eyes and his mind, girls aren't so vulnerable to such a father as boys are. I glanced at Sam, and his eyes held mine and then went neutral as he walked over to greet Olsen. The reason you have a partner is so you can glance at someone who knows. The reason *I* have a partner, anyway.

When we got to the spot, not too far off the paved road, and got out, I realized that Jouster, standing there next to the slightly battered squad car in a landscape of cacti and mesquite and subtle desert shadings, looked like a large, fancy powder puff, and I sure missed Homer. I was trailing kidnappers with a mostly untrained and untested dog.

Dave was silent about Jouster. We hadn't seen each other for a while, so he knew nothing about why there was suddenly a dog like that in my kennel, with a tracking harness on to boot. If Dave had to bet on which breeds he least expected to find me trusting with real work, he'd sure include White German Shepherds. But when I said I'd gotten him on a movie commission, he just looked at Jouster and said, more to himself than to me or the dog, "Well, I guess we haven't much to lose. At least it looks like he's got enough room in that head for some brains, even if they aren't organized, and it's always good to have one of your dogs along, Di."

That's where I had to add to the list of Jouster's insufficiencies by explaining that in addition to being a color the kidnapper could see for miles, and not having much trailing work on him, he hadn't had any man work—attack work—either.

Now that all of us were out there, in that landscape, I looked over O'Rourke and Gesner, who were, with Dave, my backup, and wondered how they would respond to a sudden difficulty. O'Rourke was one of those cops who stays looking like a bright, genial kid somewhat beyond his time, with the reddish hair to go with his name, and also that kind of substance in him that made you predict eventual promotion to detective. Also, he knew something about dogs—his dad, he said, was the assistant for a large kennel and field-trial headquarters up in Washington. I figured he would be okay.

Gesner was harder to read, as his name was harder to place. He was fair, slightly tanned, a good six feet and then some, but not heavy. He was respectful to Dave, and his eyes moved around the landscape, but whether he was reading it or just glancing around, I couldn't tell.

I used to think that tracking in the desert ought to be impossible. Any scents dry and thin immediately, and the dust gets in the dogs' noses, but I got clear on that one when I worked with old Jake Trevor, a Canadian who had become a desert rat of sorts with his dogs. He said, about the faintness of the scents, "Look. In complete silence a whisper is enough." He had turned out to be right, but it was still always awesome to me, working the dogs up there where, even though it's hardly flat desert like the Sahara, people give you directions by saying, "Turn left just past the horizon."

After Jouster had had a bit of water and a small amble on the leash, to get the kinks out, I gestured toward the interior of the Saab and gave Jouster the command. "Find It!"

Jouster took his time sniffing around in the car, even crawling into the back and checking out the floor and the inside of the rear window—not all dogs are agile enough to do this in such a tiny car. That was good, but he was a long time in the car. I had expected him to come up obviously with no result, or else to take off after something pretty fast, but he sniffed and thought and sniffed and thought over that car like a forensic chemist in a police procedural, and I couldn't get any kind of reading to speak of from him at all, only a sense so slight that it was just hope, that he really was doing *something*.

He got out and for a split second looked at me in a questioning way I couldn't read. You're closer to the sun out there, and the way his coat flashed almost distracted me from handling the tracking line.

Then Jouster moved like three police dogs in a race, and high on amphetamines to boot, and was around the Saab almost before I had finished changing my hold on the line, showing me what he looked like when he really meant an attack.

He seemed to be heading just where he was heading—toward Olsen—and Gesner instinctively put out an arm, to stop or slow him, as he almost tore the leash out of my hand, and he had Gesner pinned just long enough to stop him, and left him with a useless gun arm while he came down on Olsen, dancing around him for half a second, so that Olsen fell near Gesner.

Then he stood over Olsen, snarling, while Gesner got back to his feet. Olsen's arm later proved to have been bitten, too; no one including, I think, Olsen, noticed this for a little bit, certainly not until Olsen became able to breathe again and moved to get up.

I had gotten on Jouster almost as fast as his decision to move and was yanking him back even as he flew toward Olsen, and then I was whaling the tar out of him and thinking of all the stupid things I had said about Jouster renewing my knowledge of dogs for me. The greenest police dog in the world shouldn't make such a mistake. Of course, as far as police work went, Jouster was less than green, but a dog of even halfway satisfactory IQ and temperament should have known better than that. So much for Jouster and justice. Of course, he hadn't had any puppy conditioning with uniformed cops, but this was not all that confusing a situation, especially since Jouster had seen posse members and cops from local police departments in my classes, working their dogs and doing it in uniform.

Even afterward Jouster kept acting as though the problem was at the top of his agenda and not nearly finished, insisting that he had more work to do after he had arbitarily taken down not only a knight of justice but an innocent victim as well.

Olsen didn't look as if he really needed treatment but he was yowling, and Gesner did need to be patched, and we had, in any event, to get both of them to the hospital, to see how much of what Jouster had mashed up could be restored, though I didn't at that point care much about that, only about what I was going to do now with such a dog. He might not even be any good for movie work—the days when Rin-Tin-Tin could bite everybody on the set were long gone. The county trusted me and wouldn't insist on quarantine, but that wasn't much comfort, since I didn't look very trustworthy to myself just then.

Olsen fussed and at one point blubbered on the way to the hospital, "What if that vicious dog had gotten to my Amy?"

All I thought about then, and later at home, was that even though Jouster didn't look like trash, he was, and I hadn't tested him enough to find that out. You have a dog who bites a cop before he's even briefed, and not only that, but a cop the dog just spent two hours riding peacefully with in a car, and a dog who does that on his way to taking down the victim, and you've got a jerky cartoon where the heart and mind should be. That's what I was thinking.

The closest decent hospital was in Palm Springs, and they were thorough in determining the cause of such injuries, so there wasn't a prayer of keeping the story out of the papers, even if O'Rourke, Gesner and Olsen never decided to shoot their mouths off in a beer hall with reporters around. That meant that most of the efforts Dave and dozens of others had been for twenty years putting into getting Joe Q. Public and the city councils of the area to accept a full-fledged dog program were going to be shot to hell, and the papers would play this for all it was worth.

My dogs were acceptable only because they worked mostly

under the heading "search-and-rescue," but the papers might guarantee that I couldn't peacefully work a dog on sit-stays for a while. Anti-civil rights sentiments of those days are nothing to the anti-dog sentiment that can appear at any time at the drop of a hat, and it is never aimed at the bozos with the real man-haters but rather at good working dogs and their handlers and, most of all, at the police chiefs and councils, and the insurance companies get into the dances and lead the band and oh, hell.

Dave refrained from saying any of this to me, but I couldn't look at him.

I had misjudged Jouster. Completely. And if by then I didn't have a nose for a dog, I never would. Those thirty dogs and the woman who had them in Novato were moral giants compared to me and Jouster. At least she didn't claim to know anything about working dogs, while that's all I did, and her dogs didn't strut around looking like police-dog trackers and then bite victims.

Five hours later Gesner and Olsen were patched up and resting at home, and Olsen was presumably waiting for the midnight call. We stayed a bit with him after he calmed down, in case he had noticed something he hadn't yet remembered to tell us, but he said, "How could I remember anything? Vicious dogs are vicious dogs, and a kidnapped kid is a lost kid, and all I goddamn know is your dog who was supposed to help my Amy put me in the hospital."

When Dave droppd me and Jouster off at the kennel, I said, before I turned to go into the house, "Dave, you'll let me know what I can do."

Dave could have said, "Get Homer back into action," but he just said, "Right, Di. We'll keep you posted. Probably Gesner and Olsen both accidentally triggered the attack. I thought Gesner could handle himself better than that." That was sweet of Dave, and I didn't ruin it by reminding him that Jouster hadn't had any formal bite work at all and didn't know the attack cues and suspect maneuvers, so there wasn't any way an attack could have been triggered. Unless with Slough, or someone like Slough, he'd been agitated, but he hadn't shown any of the signs, working with me.

Dave would do what he could to keep the repercussions down, but he was a county official, and he had to set in motion a lot of the forces that would destroy his own work. He had spent his life on dog programs, the last three years working his ass off to get one in Jurupa, and Homer's work and before Homer's Duke's and Zeus', had been the mainstay of his arguments.

It was well into the darker part of the night. Luke was in the living room with Prince, both of them on the couch, Luke playing a game of pretending to be clumsy and dropping things, and Prince was darting to pick them up, scolding Luke fiercely as he did so.

And *Homer* was there, not as perky as usual, but better and, most of all, *there*. All I could see properly was Homer, as Luke got up, grabbing both Prince and me to him.

"Hey, hey, Diane! Homer's going to be okay. He's got a pulled muscle probably, at least nothing shows on the X rays, and infection started in the wake of the virus, but the tetracycline started to work right off. Homer will be fine! The vet called and Sam picked him up, Sam will tell you about it."

I tried to rejoice, and I did feel relieved as I numbly wondered why the gods were letting me off the hook even that much, but of course it wasn't Homer who had done anything dumb, just me.

Then Luke pulled back and tossed Prince toward me, saying, "Meet the relay dog! Sam says he's fast enough to make the Superdog team, at least as an alternate; his time is better than the Whippet's. Right, pooch?" I caught Prince and laughed— this much was something—and Prince barked at the ceiling and probed my neck delicately but also hard, jabbing his nose precisely against my jawbone, urging celebration.

I stood there fondling Prince, Jouster looking as noble as ever beside me, and when Luke asked me to tell him about my day with the posse, I felt as if I might cry, and also as if I had better go talk with Sam. So I said a situation had come up, and that I needed to discuss it with Sam while it was fresh in my mind.

There was Sam, and there was Lion, who sniffed and then backed off to allow us in, offering welcome while Jouster leaned with all his strength against my leg, and I just stood there and started talking. After a few sentences Sam had said, "Come on, sit down," and I sat down and kept talking, I don't know how long, not long, but after a while I realized that I was sobbing and was at the end of my story.

Sam got out food and water dishes for Jouster, who had just about had it, too, from the excitement and the fatigue of the drive, on top of the work he'd been getting. Then he took me to his couch and held me, and that's all that happened for a while until he said that the kennel work had lightened up with five dogs going home that day, and Freddie could take over more work while Sam and I worked on Jouster and live tracking. The cops, some of them, would I feel secure enough to help.

Sam said, "Well, it sounds like he just got Gesner on his way to Olsen. That's not wonderful, but it's not so bad. The question is, what was Olsen doing?"

"Nothing, Sam! He's a creep, but he wasn't doing a god-damn thing except talk to Gesner, and dammit, I really thought Jouster was thinking when he was working the car, but he wasn't."

Sam didn't argue, just said, "What do you know about this case?"

"What I've told you, what Dave told you." I leaned back and closed my eyes, and saw Luke's face. Maybe Luke was right, I should get out of this business. Maybe I should grow up and think about graciousness. Maybe I was obsessed, didn't see the danger for what it was, maybe there was no meaning, nothing to justify the risks. There was obviously nothing to my so-called judgment of a dog, and maybe Luke would be kind enough not to mention that.

I said, "We were wrong about Jouster."

Sam sat next to me and put his arm around my shoulders. "I don't think so, Annie. We don't get that wrong. He would have gone for you or me or Luke or Freddie if we were wrong. Annie, we don't get that wrong."

Luke would think differently. Luke just saw a series of dog bites and ugliness, and I had thought and said and screamed at Luke that dog bites weren't what mattered, and I had thought but didn't know how to say that what mattered was knowing the heart of the universe in the hearts of dogs, or something like that, I couldn't phrase it now to myself, because there had never been anything to phrase, really. I had wondered if Luke knew. He didn't, because there was nothing to know.

And then Sam held me some more, and left once or twice. Once must have been to go get Luke, because he arrived with some brandy and a glass and put it in my hand, and I told Luke what had happened. It took longer than to tell Sam because Luke didn't know what everything meant, and while I talked and the brandy encouraged me, my mind was suddenly busy constructing unlikely backgrounds and circumstances that would justify Jouster's attack. None of them held water long enough to think it through, much less say it. So I didn't say anything in Jouster's defense. I didn't say the bit about Jouster being trash, either.

Luke said, "So you were wrong about one dog. I've always heard, anyway, that any dog can bite. Isn't that right?"

Normally I would have said that there were bites and bites, and normally I would have said, "Not this dog, not this dog as I saw him." Normally Luke's not knowing, not knowing that he didn't know, would have mattered. But I was flat. I couldn't remember what it was that Luke didn't know. It was gone, and my bones felt thin.

Sam was a bit cross with Luke. Not having to answer remarks like, "All dogs bite, don't they?" was why he lived alone. He didn't do anything, just got so still, I could see it with my eyes closed again. He just said, sounding calm and instructorly, "There's dog bites and dog bites, Luke. Some of them mean more than others. We just don't know what this one means yet. Wish I had a chance to observe Jouster around the same group, Dave, the cops, Olsen. He might tell us something."

Sam was being kind, I thought. It was obvious what this bite meant.

Or else Luke's reservations about Sam—on the evening Sam told about Zeus in Vietnam, and Luke wondered about continuing to train dogs after that—had been right. Luke had been right to try to talk me out of the training business. That thought should have awakened me, but nothing could have awakened me.

Jouster had taken refuge with Lion, who seemed willing to welcome him into her rug in the corner.

Thirteen
MY WORDS ARE THROWN IN MY TEETH AND IT DOESN'T HELP

So Jouster was trash and a coward to boot, because he hadn't gone to work, he was too cowardly to put his mind to work in a real situation. He was trash from the moment he was whelped, or else he had been ruined by the pressure I had put on him, obviously possible since he wasn't the dog I thought I had been working, wasn't the exception to the rule about White Shepherds. I wasn't sure which reading of the situation was worse— probably the second, since if my initial judgment of Jouster had been right and I had ruined him, then I was a poor excuse for a dog trainer, indeed. My reasoning then was like that. Maybe I had been able to ruin a dog, because maybe even the Skeffingtons and the Sloughs of the world had left him with his heart intact (although his manners and grooming had needed work). He had been okay, he just wasn't the dream dog I had been inventing.

Everything I always warned my classes not to do by way of taking chances, pushing a dog, I had done, and I felt as though I didn't deserve to be on the other end of the leash from a canary. I had cotton candy instead of a trainer's mind.

I kept working the next day, even though I realized I'd have to do some fancy talking now to get the producer and director to go with Jouster after the publicity—and, indeed, Luke came in with the Jurupa, San Bernardino and Los Angeles papers. Jouster's bite didn't make it to the front page of *The Los Angeles Times*, but it did to the other two, together with the photographs of Jouster looking menacing. No doubt taken at night while we were teaching class. I had taken up classes again, and the menace was no doubt directed at the trespassing photographers, and there wasn't much else I could stand, so the next morning I just decided not to stand anything and spent an extra hour or so in bed reading the papers, with Homer, and with my arm suddenly throbbing in my consciousness like a mistake, reminding myself that there was Homer, who was getting stronger by the hour. When Luke came in to offer solace, I said that Homer was all the solace I needed. What I meant was that I just couldn't talk to anyone (unless it was Sam, but I wouldn't say that), but I didn't manage it very gently.

Luke said, "You can talk to me, Diane. You've *got* to talk to me. I love you, and besides, I really am a writer. Whatever happens between us, you've got to let me help you on this one. You've got me believing in Jouster, and if you would talk for a while I could do a feature on the posse, and not just in the desert edition."

"I can't talk. Call up Dave Buckman."

"I want you to answer my question about dog bites. I want you to tell me about a dog's judgment." He added, "And I don't want to be left out in the cold."

I saw then that he hadn't intended to say the last part, and for an instant I intended to respond as though he hadn't said it, and it would be a good idea to help him with a feature on the posse, it could save Dave Buckman's work, and while I was thinking other reasonable things, my voice said. "You don't get it. I just can't talk to you!"

Luke stiffened and said, "Yes, you don't need me for talk, or anything else. You and Sam had everything before I came along."

Amazingly he said this gently, without his eyes going ugly the way people's do, and my blood rushed along, objecting to what he had said, and I wanted to say, I don't know about Sam, but I didn't have your arms, your eyes, your mind, but I didn't say it. My arms wouldn't go out to him, my voice box wouldn't work.

He left the room, and two or three chapters went by until he returned with coffee. When he handed me my mug and sat on the edge of the bed, I felt the gentleness in every line of him, the gentleness that could give up a chance at a national name in journalism rather than misuse the power of his talent, and I was ready for anything except what he actually said. "I can't live this life, Diane, I just can't. I'm not a dog trainer. I'm not a journalist. I am writing again, writing a book because of you, but there's got to be some regularity, some . . ."

He was going to be gone. Not the way Duke, my Great Dane, and Sam's Zeus were gone, but the way thoughts are gone, the way a scent is gone and you keep being sure your dogs can pick it up again but they can't. I tried, for the sake of pride, to be angry with him for doing this at such a time and so on, but I couldn't lift a finger. He loved a woman who trained dogs, and now he was saying, "Not that shaggy," or maybe, "But not in the living room," and I was willing to groom myself if I had any idea how to do it, but I hadn't.

He said, "Your dedication frightens me." I still didn't say anything, and I didn't understand his use of the word *dedication*. It was like a word used by a tour guide in a museum; nothing to do with the reason in the shape of a sculpture.

It was my turn to say something, so I tried. I said, "I don't understand your use of the word *dedication*."

Luke's mouth tightened, so he read it as a challenge or something, and I didn't say the only other thing I could think of, which was, *I don't even know what rosewood is!* It wouldn't help. He didn't know what it was not to know that.

He sat on the bed, and then one of my arms went out to him, but the other stayed with Homer so my hand could keep rubbing the back of his ear. After a while I held him, and he held me for a while but we didn't make love, and I didn't think he'd leave, not now, not with the screening date coming up, not with all of the ruckus just about over. He didn't leave, not then. But he asked if he could move into my little spare room, at least until the day-and-night stuff with Jouster was over with, because he had trouble getting back to sleep if he woke up when I went out at night to work Jouster. I was only doing this once a night now and probably didn't need to at all, but I was doing it as though there would be occasion again for Jouster to work anywhere but in a controlled situation. That's the way I was thinking.

He was still in my arms, and I tried to imagine a regular life and drew a blank, having no idea what he was talking about. I thought perhaps I could learn it. I could try painting again. No more posse, no more chasing around on bizarre Hollywood commissions, no more upheavals. It was November by now, and the day was still cool enough so that the windows were open, and I heard Sam's voice from the training area calling, "Lion, over!" He was doing directed jumping with her.

I said, "You're leaving me, aren't you?"

Luke said, "No. No, I'm not." But he hesitated before he said it.

Luke's leaving my bed normally would have stirred up grief and a lot of efforts to eliminate the grief, such as instead eliminating the nighttime training sessions, but I already felt pretty near to dead and hopeless and had the idea that I had to save everything I had left for salvaging the situation with Jouster, at least seeing it through for the movie.

Jouster didn't scare me, not even when he talked back, as he did a bit more often after our excursion to Joshua Tree, even though he had shown me as plainly as a dog can that he had a screw loose somewhere, maybe several screws at several locations. He'd had four bites that I knew about, and I figured that the fifth and beyond would inevitably come if I again tried to use him in a situation where I trusted his judgment.

This didn't mean we couldn't use him for the movie, but it did mean that every scene had to be rehearsed pretty well, and that every actor had to be handled, too—most actors are natural bitees, and I don't mean by that they deserve it.

There was a pro forma screen test, and shooting was to begin. Not, thank heavens, on location right away, but in the studio for a week or so, so that everybody could be introduced under fairly controlled conditions. The promotion department at the studio, when consulted, said that as the film was to be a while in the making, most people would have forgotten the biting incident—Jouster didn't show up as all that *white* with the chain link throwing shadows on him, and anyway, he didn't look like himself with his face distorted against the run.

My work changed in a number of ways. Now I worked Jouster on straightforward stuff instead of both of us living at the top of our ingenuity, nailing down the control on basics. The dog had shown himself a quick study for movie routines, and I would have some time, I was told, to rehearse anything I couldn't do in ten minutes, which wouldn't be much, as long as Jouster didn't start mumbling impolitely at any actors.

Mainly I worked in public, took Jouster everywhere I could—downtown, out to the beaches, to parks, into the few bars and restaurants that allowed me in with my dogs, even into the vet's, anywhere there were strangers and action. And in a holster at my left side, slanted for easy reach by my right hand, was my rubber-coated "tranquilizer," ready to whomp him at the least sign of any aggression, and maybe I was a little whomp-happy. Fortunately, in any crowd of over five or ten people in Jurupa, there is someone who has trained a dog with me or knows about dog work somehow, so I didn't get hauled in for cruelty to animals.

Cruelty to animals! I wasn't afraid, but I handled him cautiously now. Those were no *nips* he'd given Olsen and Officer Gesner.

Dave Buckman called to say that the little girl had been returned, thanks to her grandfather's money and the restraint of the kidnapper. Child psychiatrists were working with her, but all they could come up with was that she seemed to be all right as far as her recent ordeal went. She was too young to talk or to give anyone any clues, which, as Dave pointed out, probably saved her life.

"She's a tough little thing. An experience like that! She's not quite as nonchalant as if she had just come back from a visit to Grandma's house, but near enough. She'll be okay."

"Good."

When Dave called, the publicity about Jouster was at its height, as was my lunacy. Dave was being damn generous. News of the bite had spread from coast to coast now, and whoever took that picture of Jouster behind the chain link must have been making a fortune if he was able to retain rights on it.

Dave said, "Di, couldn't we get our own shots of the dog or arrange for an interview? Jouster could play with some children. Otherwise we're just taking it lying down. At least we could be building some groundwork for the future, rebuilding public opinion."

"Dave! I don't think that would work, and anyway it looks like the dog is dangerous. You saw him! I have pretty good control, but I can't guarantee how really safe it would be, taking pictures at the children's hospital. The dog just isn't wrapped tight, and neither is his handler." I was exaggerating, thinking superstitiously; caution in the form of distrust of dogs was not my style. *And Jouster's handler is not doing anything about the fact that her man is not in her bed anymore.* Homer lay on the floor, pretty close to being well again, reading me intently.

All Dave said after a curiously long few seconds was, "All right."

I said, "What's the big deal, Dave? Homer will be well long before the next call if we're halfway lucky. He only needs a day or two, and there is Sam's new dog, Lion."

"Yeah, Sam told me he thinks she has it, but right now we need Homer and Jouster. Something's got to change fast; I'd be run out of town for using a Toy Poodle on a search, one of yours, anyway, who was inexperienced. Jouster's got to work again. Even the dog people think he's vicious because so many White Shepherds are spooky. We need Homer, and we need PR with Jouster—right now."

"How do you know Jouster isn't vicious? He bit a victim."

The phone was silent, and then Dave said, "Because he's your dog, that's why. And we need him on the team." Dave's hesitation was my cue to demand to know what was going on, but I knew that there was to be a trade-off—I would get information if I agreed to a public appearance for Jouster. The kidnapping case was more interesting than Dave had told me, and I wanted to know, but I didn't want to take any more chances with Jouster, there was the movie.

"Homer's enough! He's been on the posse for three and a half years now; he's a town hero! The Jurupa Enterprise celebrates his birthday, and so do half the cops, well maybe not half, but . . ."

"Lass, I've been hassling this one for a quarter of a century now, and Homer's reappearance will help, but the best thing for every dog handler in the country right now would be a public appearance from Jouster."

"He'll be in the *movies*. What do you want?"

Dave said, "Okay. We've got to wait it out."

We hung up, and I turned to find Sam standing there, Lion beside him, off lead—Sam gets real off-lead control—and Sam said, "Hey, now, easy. Just take it easy. There's an awfully large space in between your estimate of Jouster based on these weeks of intimate work, and your estimate of him after four seconds of flurry you still don't understand."

"You didn't *see* him."

"No more than Lion saw that valley of Vietcong, but there she is, and there's Jouster and Homer too. People get hurt when you do serious work seriously. They get hurt a lot more when you don't." Sam released Lion, and she left Sam's side to bounce out the door, out and back to the runs, and put her nose through Jouster's fence, and even put her paws under it in a play gesture. Jouster did his best to respond, as what male wouldn't to that much vibrant female.

Sam started to tell me about Zeus, not only everything I'd already heard but then some, about how he was always too sharp after the Army's version of man work, which was about the only version Sam knew then, and about how if the dog is good, all that means is that you have to rethink working the dog and so on. None of this bored me.

Then I got the idea that Sam should handle Jouster, since I was about done in and all I could think of was more hours of work, and I knew with my head, though not my heart, what Sam meant about "rethinking"—not that you had to know, because there was Lion.

Later I put this idea before Luke, the two of us talking in the small, porchlike shed at the back of my house where some equipment was stored—extra leashes, collars and so on. Luke wanted to know why, instead of trying to force different loyalties on Jouster, we didn't all just cool it for a while.

"Because of the movie," I said to Luke, who was shocked. "The movie still matters, and I'm losing heart for this work with Jouster."

Luke said, "Only one trainer per dog. One per dog. You spend an hour on that in the first class, and you say it again throughout the course. One trainer per dog."

I was shocked, too, at myself. You don't just hand over the leash and a set of commands, not on any dog, but especially not on a dog like Jouster, even if Sam is the person most likely to succeed, especially not this close to a big project. There are "trainers" who make a game of training, and one of the things they do is teach a dog to do a recall in a circle of people, to anyone who calls, but that's not what a recall is. "Jouster, find it!" or "Jouster, come!" is like "I love you." It's not a transferable bond, or rather it transfers only when there is much more care, intelligence and love even than there is when our species says, "I love you."

In fact, the shock of hearing myself say, "I'm through, it's time for Sam to step in with Jouster," was great enough so that I dismissed it even before Luke had finished. I mumbled something about Sam having more experience with attack-triggered dogs than I had, and Luke demanded to know where this routine came from, and I said I didn't want anyone getting killed because of my vanity.

"Dammit! Half the Southwest can't be wrong about your

dog work. Besides, everybody dies or gets killed anyway. That's no reason to throw away life and dogs and—and love while you've got them!" Luke had turned toward something. This wasn't the Luke who talked about being afraid of my dedication, and I thought that in the last couple of weeks, since Luke had moved out of my bed, he was finding that dedication was okay from a distance. But this was still a different Luke, or rather, this was a full-fledged version of the man I had fallen in love with, but newer even than that, and I was going to ask him what Luke it was, but just then Sam walked in. I didn't know how much he'd heard, but he looked distracted, inward, and heated himself a cup of coffee on his way into the living room and the old armchair that no one used but Sam, who shared it now, briefly and grumbling, with Lion, who had developed quite a repertoire of ways to test her feminine wiles on Sam. You wouldn't have thought a dog like Lion could become capable of regality and seductiveness and at other times be almost cuddly. Sam says that's why she used to bite, that not having her regality was a deficiency, that it was part of what a bitch had to have, that she had her rights too. Sam was in love.

"Di," he said, "we've got to get some more kennel help or give up on the flick. I've got my own dog now, and I want to stay on top of her, and Freddie is about to collapse—when did you last see him teaching one of his dogs to do a new routine in his spare time? We've got, counting our own dogs, a dozen canines to work and twenty boarders, and the trainees are good and tough—half of them, anyway. And my back is breaking because I won't give up on Lion, she's turning into something."

"But aren't her people due to pick her up soon?"

Sam grinned. "Oh, right, they're back from the Côte D'Azur where they brag about this genuinely American dog they have, so I donated some extra time to showing them what they had to do to keep her steady."

I looked at him straight, but he just looked up into one of

his eyebrows. "Just like I always do. Sometimes, just once in a while, I still lay it on a little thick."

He looked at the ceiling now, and then back at his coffee, and then at Lion, who looked back happily. "I suggested they wear good tennis shoes for the first six months with Lion, until she quit trying to knock them off-balance, and said no guests for a while until they felt certain they had control . . ."

Here, Luke had yet another lesson in my and Sam's perfidy and laughed, saying, "You two are just plain dog thieves!" Or tried to say it, but Sam and I were both talking at once, and I thought maybe I'd been wrong about Jouster, but we weren't, wrong about *her*—this Lion bitch looked like coming through everything in spades. Sam even used her now—all one hundred and twenty-seven pounds of her—in his obedience classes, selecting the smallest and youngest, or else the oldest and most tottery of his students, to demonstrate exercises, having them work Lion, and she submitted to this with a gentle wit that was her Airedale rather than her hound heritage.

"I did not tell them she was dangerous," said Sam. "I just said they should get some good tennis shoes and . . ."

Now I have to say that an unfriendly observer might here have thought Sam looked excessively pleased with himself, but he was mostly that pleased with Lion.

"You know how people are. They called back later: Would I take the dog in lieu of training fees? I said I'd be willing to pay them for the dog but I said it softly—I figured they owed you something for that arm—so when they offered to pay me instead, I said, 'Oh, no. I have to finish training her before I can begin to think of finding a home for her, and someone else will pay me for the dog in time.'" We talked for a while about what kind of home.

"I didn't say anything that wasn't true," Sam said. "I told them she wasn't at the end of her novice training period yet and that she would be fine for them in a couple of weeks, as in our original contract, which is true. "But you know, it's hard to find a good home for a big, rough dog like that. They insisted on forking over, and I gave the money to Rita, who needs it for vet bills for the pet-rescue work she does.

"But now it's time to think seriously about either pulling out of that movie or finding more help. We have the money, and it's ridiculous being so ass-tired all the time that you can't work your own dog. Homer and Lion have a deeper claim on us than Hollywood does."

Homer came and stood by me, and when Jouster's hackles raised ever so slightly, Lion got up and licked his neck and withers until they went down, and he was calm again. For a minute I was wishing Lion were a purebred something.

"Okay," I said. "Ask Freddie to go through recent class records and locate himself an assistant. We'll increase his pay and give him a percentage, and he can manage his hourly help as he likes. A woman, maybe—someone who doesn't mind grooming. The kennel is beginning to look like the location of the punch line of a shaggy-dog story."

I said it because it was the only way to keep in shape with Jouster for the movie, and because I could probably work things around so that Luke might want to come back to my bed. But it was Sam Luke looked at.

Then Luke—the new Luke—moved back a few steps for effect and said, "Yes, leave it to Freddie and Blue. He's good PR for you, you know. It was Freddie who sent me to you with Prince. I did a story on the two of them when they started patrolling the little park next to Freddie's dad's house."

"Patrolling a park?" I said. I hadn't known about this, and I was worried at the idea of a sixteen-year-old kid and a Coonhound taking on anything in the way of criminals. "What park?"

Luke said, "It seems to have started by accident. Blue was already a competent Open dog, retrieving over hurdles, broad jumps and so on, and had started Utility-level directed retrieving, jumping, scent discrimination, hand signals, everything—

enough to raise my consciousness. Freddie used to work him in Handfield Park, a little triangle of grass, with a tree or two, and he taught Blue the old seek-back exercise, just for the hell of it, and then Blue started on his own picking up lost wallets and keys and things, so Freddie, together with a cop who came by on regular patrol once in a while, set up a little lost-and-found, and then what Freddie told me was that Blue's eyes started getting really yellow and dangerous when someone tried to get something or do something that wasn't in their sphere. And the cop started coming by unofficially at around the same time Blue and Freddie Kubie were out there, like an unofficial backup, and they caught a few people that way who were pretty far from being nice to talk to. Fred said you taught him how to do it."

That was alarming. "I did?" I only remembered the pair doing well in my classes.

"He took a hint from one of your spiels about police and protection and search work, about dogs knowing what doesn't go where, so he started seeing what Blue would do if he followed him on a loose "okay" command, and Blue turned out to redirect his—and Freddie's—desire for raccoon hunting into a less bloody interest in keeping the park safe when they could. Di, are you *sure* you don't know about this? It was the cop who got a detective who got someone who got my editor on to it, and I was sent to do the story. Page-and-a-half feature, with photos. Color."

I shook my head.

"I wondered what he wanted to do—go into the movies, maybe? A dog like that! He said, 'No. Maybe sometime.' Right then he was busy being a housekeeper and keeping the dirt backyard tidy and clean so Blue could jump there safely. I said that training Blue to do all of those things was quite an accomplishment; how had Freddie done it? He told me it was none of *his* doing, it was just that the best dog trainer in the world happened to live nearby, and she had taught him what to do.

"I wondered where in the world the kid—the young man—

had found the heart to do all of that without any help, and I wondered even more after the feature was done, and there I was training Prince, and it took more heart than I had, just about. . . . So that's why now I'm finding it so hard to see you wasting your heart on Jouster and this movie, when you don't have to kill yourself to train—it was different when you still thought Jouster had it, but now you say he's no good. . . ."

Here Sam roared up out of his chair like a hound of hell, which was how I learned that there was more something or other between those two than I had thought.

"Luke, goddammit, you haven't paid the slightest bit of attention. Do you have to have everything collapse on you four times before you begin to get it? Now come outside with me, and I'll give you one more chance before I call every honest Humane Society in the country on you for even thinking such thoughts in the presence of a good dog like Jouster! Sir, if you please!?"

It wasn't *Luke* who had said anything against Jouster, and I puzzled over it. Luke grinned at Sam's anger, and they walked out with Lion between them, leaving me and Jouster and Homer with loose, stupefied jaws.

I had to get Jouster ready. I didn't have time to find out what it was all about, so I went out to the runs and the kennel office for jumps and equipment, put them in the Toyota with Jouster and headed for the police station where the chief had said I could work Jouster as long as I could guarantee quiet and safety for the civilians and everyone else. It was time for training. Time for a little PR too.

Jouster was still breathtaking, moving as true as a dog with a real heart does, but the more beautiful Jouster was, the less I wanted to see him glow. Could the movie be true if the dog wasn't? Was the dog true, after all? Whether or not he was, I decided, he looked good. He had never stopped looking good, and there was still a chance that at last there would be a true movie about the power a good dog carries as casually as beauty carries silk.

Before I got in the car to go downtown I had started to walk back to the cottage, intending to say this to Luke, and to try to say that I was with him, but I could see his outline, working at the small table in the room he now slept in, and turned around, to work the dog. Jouster was excited by my uneven turns and leapt at my side for a moment or two, holding the leash in his mouth with a gaiety I couldn't doubt but did.

Fourteen
BUT
JOUSTER
REFUSES
TO STOP
GLOWING

Freddie took to his new duties so well, it was hard to notice he hadn't always had them. He had found Bethany Jo—Jo, she liked to be called—who was delighted to be working part-time at minimum wage, who had had a dog in one of Sam's classes, a Golden Retriever who had died early of a degenerative bone disease, so she was saving up for a new dog but didn't have anything to save until Freddie offered her the job. She was also saving for a set of hurdles and bars and broad jumps and all of the rest of it, and was naturally good and careful in her work.

We cleaned out the old trailer that had been the kennel

office, and Freddie moved in. I overheard Freddie talking to Jo one day about the Nordic breeds, because she so admired George that she was wanting a Samoyed.

He had known her Golden, so he said, "See, Jo, you're used to a dog who's smart and loyal in the same part of him. A Nordic is smart and he loves you, but if you go for a walk, he'd just as soon stay out and be smart for a day or two and several miles away."

He correctly figured that if she had had a working Golden, a Samoyed wouldn't be right for her, and so although he was obviously still entranced by George, he was repeating bits of an early conversation I'd had with him about George. Freddie was large enough in the heart to adore two kinds of dog at once and to work them, but I hadn't known that when he first showed up with George, which is why I had tried to talk him out of committing himself to the dog. I pointed out that with virtually all of the Nordic breeds you're going to run into a loyalty problem.

"What do you mean, ma'am?"

"Don't call me that!" Freddie had stood there, all freckles and red hair, with no capacity in him for misery, and his genius for dogs, and I was just starting to feel impatient with his funny, quaint formality. Like everything about Freddie it was cheerful and sui generis.

"What do you mean about a loyalty problem, D-D-d-diane?"

"Well, George here is an eyeful, all right, especially the way you've been keeping his coat and exercising him, and you could probably, if you had some papers on him, get a breed championship, if my eye is halfway reliable. But he'll take off, split; you'll never know whether or not he'll be there when you turn to make contact with him out in the hills—or downtown, for that matter."

George was, in fact, a more than merely acceptable representative of his breed, sturdily built, with that winning way most Sammies have of always seeming to be smiling, and something else in him, suggestive of Arctic visions, made me see why there is a debate about what the word *Samoyed* means. Some people say it means "self-consuming" and add that early explorers brought extra dogs and fed the weaker dogs to the stronger ones when the trail got rough. Others say it means "self-sustaining," the way the North Star is.

But who gives a damn about having the North Star around the house? Who would want to command it? Who *could* command it?

"Well," Freddie told me, "Blue is as loyal as three or four dogs. I think I want something showy too. I never had anything showy before—Blue is genuine, of course. My uncle said I could have him if he got killed. He did get killed—I don't think he expected to—and Blue was mine, and then I trained him with you, and he was really mine. I never had anything showy, and I tried for two months to find George's owners because he was a stray, and if I can't find any coons, I might want to go sledding up in the mountains."

I forgot that Freddie lived as deeply and happily in the formalities of the breeds, traditions and legends and all, as if he weren't an orphan with no knowledge of his own history. It wasn't sledding that mattered, it was the form of the dogs. "Blue is perfectly capable of pulling a sled."

"That wouldn't be right. I mean, I'll teach him to pull in case I need him, just like I'll teach George to retrieve and scent, but it isn't what he's for. He's not a mushing dog, he's a coon dog."

"Okay, but with the Nordics you've got to remember that just because a dog is hardheaded, it doesn't mean he knows anything. And it's going to be a long, slogging job to get off-lead control."

"Yes, uh, Diane. But sled dogs don't have to work off-lead."

About six weeks later it dawned on me with what delicacy Freddie had stayed away from the obvious difficulty, which is that without money, you choose from among the stray, vaga-

bond, and delinquent classes of dog, or else orphans left behind
by your relations.

Plainly there had been nothing I could do about Freddie,
and more to the point, nothing I ought to do about him. Also, I
now told myself, you were a fine one to talk, you who are putting
everything you've got and risking Luke and Sam and the kennel
and Homer and God knows what else for that Jouster dog, who's
worse than any Nordic could ever be, a sneaking, dishonest dog,
a dog who bites out of goddamn juvenile punk pride and does
so with a child's life at stake. I believed this despite even Sam's
faith in Jouster, still felt compelled and confused by Luke's
questioning.

He had done it with me at stake, too, I could have added
but didn't. There was that much of a dog trainer left in me, that
I didn't figure Jouster owed me my fantasies.

It became time for another trip to Malibu, to settle finally
the initial logistics of the movie. I had said to Kaye earlier that
I'd like to keep the dog and work him myself in front of the
cameras, instead of training and finding fees. Kaye was grumpy
about that, because this was to be his comeback, and even though
he would be on the picture as head animal trainer, he had
wanted it to be a complete comeback, but he didn't have much
choice, not because my position was morally or legally impreg-
nable but rather because Kaye really was a trainer still, and he
knew that it wasn't money that made a dog belong to someone,
especially a German Shepherd, of whatever color. Now I thought
of offering Jouster to Kaye again, to work himself, and would
have, but with each such thought my mind lurched in rebellion.
That part of me that believed in Jouster objected to this—Jouster
wasn't Jack Kaye's dog.

Kaye, when we got there, was beyond such possibilities, and
beyond the movie too. We showed up at seven-thirty A.M., hoping
to beat his breakfast tequila to his mind, but we didn't make it.
He seemed amiably puzzled to see us and called us "my dears" a
lot, but he didn't seem to recognize Jouster.

He was edging toward the weepy part, so we let him weep, and in weeping, he became for a while coherent, after the first few minutes of uncontainable sobs. The producer had pulled out—panicked, Kaye said—because the scriptwriter had pulled out, and without that writer, the director had pulled out.

Sam took notes all this time, writing, writing, writing, gallantly planning, I was sure, to find a script, director and star to play across from Jouster. There he sat with his notebook on his lap, his intelligence never losing stride, extracting from Kaye's ramblings the names of everyone who had been interested in the movie. Not for immediate use, but just because Sam's like Lion, a terrier, he stays with it.

He said, "Has the writer really pulled out?"

Kaye said, "He had to, he's got to eat, and he had a chance to rewrite the story for Universal; Wildcat gave him back the option, had to when they broke contract."

After a bit, however, even Sam plainly thought it was time to leave, but I thought I'd better talk to Kaye some more. It was too much, after everything, just to let it go like that. I decided I would stay, sober Kaye up, find the heart I figured he still had, have him work Jouster. He'd come through, I was telling myself, against all of the evidence. He would have to come through. There are more real scriptwriters south of Bakersfield than there are good dog handlers. We could have a contest for the script, I thought wildly.

I had a quiet confab with Sam about this; Sam figured I was crazy, but training partners are as loyal to each other as real dogs are. So Sam shrugged agreement and support as he watched Kaye shambling around the room. Even Pierre seemed to have given up on Kaye, who, to his credit, registered the fact that the dog was not cowering away from his drunkenness, was not afraid, but too full of love to acknowledge this inept travesty of his master and partner. A Bouvier's heart is pretty hard to break, but it can be broken by too much travesty, and I was anxious for Pierre, who started back every time Kaye gave out one of those little giggles at some internal or remembered joke.

I told Sam I wanted some time alone with Kaye.

Sam thought about it and said, "Maybe it will work, if you can do the womanly bit; maybe it really was his wife's dying that broke him." I had forgotten that.

Sam drove into old downtown L.A., where there was a shop that must have been there when the Spaniards arrived, where you could get any shape, grain or size of any kind of leather, beautifully stitched and fitted; he wanted that Lion dog to have her own harness, from a pattern he had made. The one he was using on her was adjustable, and I didn't see how a new harness could be more comfortable, but these are the little romances bitches, when they're any good, enjoy having with their trainers, if the trainer is any good. Kaye became mindlessly expansive again and sent his chauffeur and limo to save Sam bus fare and/or parking problems.

I took charge of Kaye, knowing less than a dust devil about what it was to do that. I gathered up all of the booze and balanced it on top of the curtain rods. Pierre (and Jouster, too, to give him his due) seemed to realize what this would mean if Kaye wanted a drink, and after the first four or five bottles, they brought me the others, one at a time. I took the phone off the hook and turned off all bells and buzzers that I could find.

Then I stood in front of Kaye. He kept shifting his gaze away from me, but I kept moving back into it, both dogs with me, Jouster on the left in normal working position, Pierre on the right. Kaye must have taught him that, probably for a scene some director demanded and then didn't print.

All I said was, *"Blaze. Algonquin. Riddles. Algonquin. Brag Dog. Algonquin. Jerry of the Islands. Algonquin. Treve. Algonquin. Rough Gold. Algonquin."*

Algonquin was Kaye's greatest movie. The dog work was spectacular, but Kaye's dog work was always spectacular. "In *Algonquin*," one critic said, "the acting was transcendent, the script played as though it had been made for exactly the best in that bunch of human and canine actors, the director's vision was never false and the cameramen gave the director more than the director could have dreamed of." *Variety* gave a major headline to its box-office success.

Jouster's unstable character turned out to be handy at one point. Kaye was stumbling in my general direction, his arms held out in boozy amorousness, and Jouster got him in the leg. A nip rather than a bite, but a nip that would be a week or so fading. Jouster would have to be watched even more carefully than I had thought; he ought to be able to distinguish a harmless drunk from someone genuinely threatening. I figured, even though I was relieved not to have to wrestle Kaye off, weak as he was.

Kaye read it as the gods tapping him on the shoulder. He went back to one of the ten-foot couches and sat down, saying, "Goddamn. I'll be goddamned. Hey, dog, would you teach Pierre some of your stuff? Come on over here, show me what you got, uh—what's his name?"

"Jouster."

He practiced doing the syllables a few times under his breath before he tried it aloud, then got it right the first time.

"Jouster, you ought to be in movies, eh?" Here he reached out his hand, to wave Jouster closer, and I got over there fast, Kaye being in no shape to deal with an unpredictable biter. But Jouster walked over to him and submitted to intoxicated, but apparently not, for him, toxic caresses with voice and hands. The dog was even worse than I'd thought; going over to be nuzzled at the request of a drunk he had just bitten made him the only genuinely, wholly unpredictable biter I had ever known. The reason I hadn't answered Luke's questions about Jouster's aggressiveness was because there wasn't any answer. I hadn't until that moment really believed in a congenitally dishonest dog.

I said to myself, *Well, Diane, this is what you've put at the center of your universe. A dog that would first bite a harmless drunk and then eagerly accept the mindless slobberings of said drunk.*

Then came the part that I had forgotten is supposed to get written into any crummy, behind-the-scenes history. Kaye was a bit more sober now and started talking somewhat coherently about how, if I went to bed with him, we might, just might, be able to salvage the movie. Sentimental nonsense, but any port in a storm, except that Luke was part of the storm, and so far with Luke I had only been an idiot. Betrayal was something else. Besides, even if there wasn't much to Jouster, there was still a lot to the *idea* of Jouster, and the movie, and it was Jouster's image that kept me talking about Kaye's dogs, kept that bit of nonsense out of my life. If Kaye's return of confidence depended on a lay with me, it wasn't going to happen.

So I just kept talking, about my idea of why the movie mattered, about what we could do with Jouster in front of a camera, about not giving up, about all of that. The kitchen had decaffeinated instant in it, so I served him coffee while I talked. When he got genuinely sober, he looked even more of a wreck than when he'd been drunk, but he was talking differently now.

You can risk your reason for knowledge, but I couldn't think of the question whose answer was me in bed with Kaye. Kaye seemed to have good questions with that answer, but I thought about Jouster, who would, of course, have made no sense of the situation at all if I had done that. I was still promising Jouster that this was a working life, and as I had said to Luke, everything is the dog trainer's responsibility.

On the drive home I thought of telling Luke about Kaye's pass, about the way my mind kept honoring Jouster by putting the dog's image before me like that, but Luke might have expected to talk more about how it had been his image, and I then wouldn't know how to say that I believed I could be loyal to Luke and still think of what the work meant, and I remembered Sam saying maybe he should have been a monk.

Fifteen
A BEAR
AND AN
ELEPHANT
AND
FREDDIE

When I got home and reported the basics of the day to Luke, I was surprised to find him responding, even responding with momentum, "The movie will get made. If not that movie, then another movie, and you will be able to show what Jouster is."

This was the new Luke. I started to speak, but Luke went on. "I got hold of a copy of that script, you know. One of the things I did when I was a struggling young journalist was to write movie reviews, and I didn't feel I could do it well unless I consulted the script, at first, so I learned how to get scripts and how to read them. This one is unfinished, but not bad."

■

Close to two months went by, with no scenes between me and Luke, but with him staying in the spare room. I backed the pressure off Jouster and spent time building the business so as to make full use of Freddie and Jo, drummed up enough new Saturday afternoon students so that Freddie was teaching his own novice class and put Jo to work for the hell of it making statistical sense of the information we had collected on thousands of dogs and handlers over the past eight years. I had had some hunches about the relationship between higher education and dog blindness that I wanted to check out. I was right, as it turned out, not that there's anything intrinsically wrong with intellectuals, but most of them get going too fast because there is something intrinsically wrong with the reasoning process, and then you put people in a university, where there's nothing to slow them down, so their minds freewheel and they can't work dogs.

Jouster actually got a small stand-in part. Jack Kaye called up and said they needed a Shepherd to do a rescue scene with a bear, and Jouster was the only dog he knew of off-hand who was gutsy enough to do the scene.

I asked Kaye what was wrong with Kaye himself doing it with any one of the good Shepherds he must have access to. Kaye said, "Not a thing wrong with the Shepherds out there. It's the old man who can't work bear, or much of anything else for a little while here. You see, your Jouster, when he nipped me— never knew a dog who had such a precise vocabulary, no waste of energy in that nip and no resentment or miserliness about it, either—well, there have been other things in my life, but I'm a dog trainer, and when I'm really down on my psychic luck, it's got to be a dog who brings the message. Right now, kid, Jack Kaye can't work a dog or a bear. I'm technically dried out a month and a half now, but my mind will take longer. I can feel it, and I owe it to the dogs not to go working them in a big-game scene without being ready myself to make the right maneuvers. You and Jouster, though, you'll be fine."

"Where is it set?"

"Arkansas or Mississippi or someplace. Everything in it is around hunting, so you have the Shepherd and the hunting hounds and the terriers."

"Do you have a lead hound?" I was thinking of Lion, of course.

"No, none of the dogs are even from hunting lines; we're going to have to fake that with estrogen. Got a bunch of show hounds is all, but I'll lay out that estrogen, get them sniffing the ground like they loved God."

"You want a real hunting hound?"

"What do you think you have?" Kaye asked cautiously. He was, for that moment at least, all dog trainer. I told him about Lion, and he perked up, talked about how his scriptwriter could easily write in a real character for her. And I called Sam, and it turned out, naturally, that he had taught Lion about three times as many routines as they could possibly need, so she would have a tryout.

I perked up a little. It was hardly *the movie*, of course, or even a real role for Jouster, but it was something, it would get Jouster up in front of a fair number of people, even if he was to be in disguise.

What Jouster had to do was double for a black-and-tan Shepherd (we had to dye him) who was playing the part of the noble dog, but they couldn't get the Shepherd they had anywhere near the bear, so there was just the one scene they wanted Jouster to do. This was to be filmed on a ranch up above Santa Barbara.

It was a tricky business, and I suppose if anyone but old Jack Kaye had called, I would have refused; you don't go risking a mauling by a real live bear just to jazz up a slow part of the story line in a movie, at least I don't. Besides which, surely there were enough black-and-tan Shepherds in Southern California, especially in the Hollywood Dog Obedience Club, who could and would do it. But I said Jouster and I would do it.

Louie Gerard was doing the wild animal work for the film, and after I talked to Kaye, I called him. He said that even though of course Kaye's word on a working dog was irrefutable, he wanted to watch the dog work, and would I bring the dog by the training compound the next morning at seven-thirty?

I showed up at six-thirty instead, to give Jouster time to sort out and analyze all the wild-animal smells and noises in the grassy center of the main compound. It was like a gigantic, not very well-kept lawn, fenced in by cages and enclosures of all sorts and more kinds of wild animals than you could count. Any dog is more likely than not to blow his cool the first time a wolf or a Galapagos tortoise insults him, so I gave Jouster a chance to check the place out. I was worried about whether or not he would come through; a dog who will bite a victim and then a perfectly harmless drunk is likely to fail you when you need real guts and substance from him. But he had that presence, and Sam believed in him, so there we were.

Louie knew a thing or two himself, so he was figuring that I would do just what I did, get there early so that he wouldn't see it if the dog freaked out. That's why he showed up early too. While I was unloading Jouster, I heard a cheerful "Good morning!" and I knew that now the only thing to do was to go ahead as if Louie weren't there.

I took a chance and didn't even try to work up to the tricky stuff by degrees, just called Jouster to heel, and we walked out into the middle of it all. After a few minutes the general tang of wild-animal compound separated into distinct smells. The tang of the pumas was there, the sulky musk of the wolf, the various, somewhat damp reeks of the monkeys and apes, the royal scent of the elephants, the warm sweetness of the antelopes, llamas and zebras, each of these with its own resonance. There was a medley of noises but subdued; the native birds of the desert valley of Jurupa were the only ones who had anything but quiet comments to make on the early morning.

Jouster quivered with delighted bother. He was especially

worried about the wolf, although the wolf wasn't making any noise and the Bengal tiger was getting restless. Most of the cages, including the wolf's, were set on cement-block platforms eighteen to twenty-four inches high. It was the wolf's cage I walked up to and stood by for a moment. Louie, I knew, would be watching intently, but I made myself unaware of him and concentrated. Jouster was sitting at heels beside me, and we were no more than a leash length away. The wolf was of at least two minds about what to do about this. On the one hand, he ought to be defending something, and on the other, there was the fencing he couldn't get through.

In the two or three seconds during which the wolf was sorting out his options, Jouster was studying the wolf.

At that instant I sent him to fetch the dumbbell, which I had leaned against the cement foundation of the cage. Jouster got about halfway there and then suddenly fled back to me, nearly jumping into my arms.

The second time he made himself get close enough to where his muzzle touched the dumbbell, and then he crouched and peed before he tried to run back to me. Now I knew why we have the phrase "yellow coward." Not that *this* was Jouster's cowardice; I was throwing two continents worth of alien life at him, and for a moment his system was simply overloaded. I hope I never get that scared, but I wasn't taking anything at all from Jouster that morning. I threw the dumbbell a third time, and this time he got it just fine, even if he did start out a bit cautiously, dropping his neck down between his shoulder blades after looking back at me to see if I would offer an out. And he brought it back faster than the god of thunder's favorite boomerang, came through for me in spades.

Louie was impressed, and so was I, but I acted as if we hadn't even met a challenge yet. The biggest Bengal tiger was about thirty feet from the wolf, with some macàques in between, so I mosied on past the macàques and tossed the dumbbell over by the bottom of the tiger's cage.

Jouster had worked out a few things at this point, Jouster-style, and he went in solidly after that, with the Bengal hitting his cage ten or twelve feet up and screaming and roaring like a professional—all right, he *was* a professional—a racket too unreal and wild-sounding for the movies coming out of him, and Jouster was back with the dumbbell, slick as you please, calmly sitting in front of me holding it and wagging his tail. Well, I loved the dog, biter or no.

The tiger didn't calm down, though. The next time I sent Jouster, he got about four feet from the big cat and, instead of going for the dumbbell, went for the tiger with righteous murder blazing from him. He hit the tiger's cage about eight feet off the ground, at about the same level as the cat's jaws, and fence or no fence, I think he would have taken down the cage and clearly intended to take down the kitty, but I had the leash and stopped him hard all the while I was cheering silently, and got on his ear. The next time he went, scooping up the dumbbell with as much authority as you'll ever see, with the cat trying to take the chain link and cement apart twelve inches from the dumbbell. And the next time he got it, and the next time, and then I had him do signal exercises between two lion cages about eight feet apart, and he moved as accurately and as calmly as a dancer there, with the lions leaping and roaring insults on both sides of him.

Louie started jumping around and almost lost his cool in an untrainerish fashion, saying to the handlers and keepers who were by now showing up for the day's work that Jouster was the hottest working dog you *ever* saw, and it suddenly made me feel sick at heart, that there could be a dog like that who not only fooled me but fooled Sam, and now this nice guy, Louie. But he would be okay for the bear scene, and of course he got the job. Louie wanted to handle him, but I said I handled my own dogs, which is true, but mainly I didn't want to have to explain to Louie that "the hottest goddamn working dog you *ever* saw" had a screw loose somewhere.

It was sometimes hard for me to remember this, especially when he worked like that.

When I got back and told Luke about it, I forgot that I didn't love Jouster, and Luke wanted to know if that didn't perhaps show that he was the hottest goddamn working dog I *ever* saw. He wanted to know this affectionately, and he actually wanted to know it, he wasn't taunting me. I didn't know what had changed. We had both been working, Luke on the book, whatever it was, and we had backed off, trying to explain ourselves to each other, just as well, and somewhere in the two months we had switched places so that now I was the one not believing in dogs.

"Look, I've already had a fair go at believing that stuff myself, and my believing it put one innocent man in the hospital and may have ruined Dave's work on getting a dog program in this county. I have already muffed it about as badly as I can. Anyway, I probably ruined him, and I don't intend . . ."

We had been quiet together, and Luke was cheering Jouster on, but there wasn't enough ease between us for that. Luke turned, stiff, called Prince to heel and went out, no doubt to sit on his favorite thinking rock, about a half a mile from the kennel. He liked to say that several landscapes met there, so he could think better when he was writing. He was spending an inordinate amount of time up on that rock lately, instead of working in the kitchen, so I'd messed it up with him, too, and maybe even worse than I'd thought. Luke had stopped talking about his writing to me, and even though the sunlight, when it got tangled in his eyes, made the lashes shine across his whole face, I was too comfortable with him living in the other bedroom.

I thought, *I would be ashamed for Sam to know. Something is wasted here.* So I walked out to the rock and didn't take Jouster, who was in the kennel run, or Homer, who for an instant thought I meant him to go, but then decided not. Luke would have Prince with him, but I would start talking about training if

I took a dog, and I wanted to talk about Luke. I was beginning to feel that maybe life without proper human love was insufficient no matter how the dogs work. And I thought for a while by thinking about Luke's body, his body was direct and passionate, you could feel the whole man in his body and movements, and these days, when I saw him writing, I could see the whole man curved into a single thought as he worked. I wondered if now, after two months of quiet, if he came back into my bedroom . . .

So I apologized to Homer, who settled on the rug under the kitchen table to wait. If you have dogs and care about them, that happens. They have to wait.

Luke was bent over a notebook when I came close, and he didn't notice me, so I waited for him to pause, hoping that he would know why I was there, and say something first. Even though I knew that if he did guess why I was there, he wouldn't be likely to say something first.

Eventually he did look up and see me, and I walked over to where he could give me a hand climbing up next to him. From his perch the symmetry of the cottages, the kennel and the training grounds was easy to see: the cottages balancing each other and the runs behind them balanced on each side by grassy training areas that ran back to the undeveloped ground behind the kennel, which itself was partially divided by the quite weedy cow pasture that occasionally housed someone's cow or horse temporarily.

"I don't much like the way things are right now," I said, putting my hand on his hand where it rested on his leg, holding the pen. That hand just kept to itself while the other one set down the notebook. That was far as I was to get on why I was there.

"No," he said. The hand I was touching slipped out gently so my own hand went to rest on my own leg, and he started playing with his pen, shifting it from one hand to the other. I didn't know what that no was made out of, but it wasn't very inviting, and nothing else came out of my mouth for a while. I smelled the sweet and busy brush and listened to the insects' complicated humming as they maintained the portion of the earth given to them.

After a while Luke said, "I wanted to write real *stories*. Fiction. I'm writing one now, and it won't end up with the others. In that box. Someone will want it. When I fell for you, I wasn't consciously wanting a woman. I wasn't consciously wanting much, but I couldn't let go of the idea of real work. I thought, though, that I had given that up when I gave up journalism. I gave it up, and I was happy on Esther's ranch, because that was real and she was real, and I didn't think much after a while about writing.

"This is real," he said, the curve of his arm taking in the kennel as a whole. I could just make out Sam, or a speck that was probably Sam, in the training area with the hurdles, working one of Roy Rogers' Setters. Sam mostly didn't have any use for actors, but he liked Rogers, who was interested in field trials. "And I love you. Loving you—mostly for a while by bumping my shins against you, I suppose—has given me back, not the old kind of writing, which no editor wants these days, anyway, but my *work*. And this book," he said, turning the notebook over so I couldn't see, "is for you if it comes out okay. But you don't love me the way I love you, and if you knew how I love you, you'd go nuts. I moved out of your bed so that I didn't have to lie there restless every night because I couldn't do anything about loving you except lie there. I couldn't even comfort you after the episode with Jouster and Olsen, so I had to move out of your bed, but I couldn't go any further, and couldn't get any closer, couldn't talk with you about training, about the dogs."

"You can talk about training with me perfectly well! Or writing, or anything else you like."

"Yes, but these days I don't much. I can hand out encouragements, but I really don't know, not why, but how all of this matters to you. I love Prince, and you and he showed me the way back to something real, the places where the going is just rough enough and leads somewhere, but Prince is still—well, working on relay races is fun, even joyous, but it's not working with bear, and it's not twenty-four hour training stints. I can do that, maybe, just maybe, if I have to for a book, once in a while, but not as a way of life, and not with dogs. Those stints are not my ways, I have ways, but they aren't it."

I was desperate and started to say, "But I've always got room for a partner who doesn't do that," but of course I already had a partner, and now I wished for a second that I had stayed below with Sam—he had asked me if I had time to do some distracting for him that afternoon. For no reason I remembered the fifth or sixth time I'd worked with Sam. We both had had classes, and had been using each other's classes as places to work our own dogs, and we were both at the tail end of confused love affairs. Afterward we met some of our students for coffee, to discuss specific problems, or shows, or just to shoot the bull, and that evening Sam had said, "Why don't we go for a glass of wine instead?" That would have led to bed, and I was willing, but I was also quite suddenly determined not to ruin my friendship with this man, and it seemed pretty clear at the time that love and working friendships didn't go together in my life. So I'd said I had to get to bed early.

I took myself back to the present and said, as I moved over for Luke to hold me, which he did, "How much do you have to do on the book?"

He sighed. "I can't really tell yet. I'll know soon just where it's going, I think."

Then I said, because it was true, "I've got to make a call about this little scene with the bear." I started to say, "I'll miss you," but that would have been dumb, like a soap opera, and it was close to suppertime. Thanks mostly to Sam, we still had a suppertime.

At the kennel, Freddie was working George. He had seen that for movies, George, with his wit and his sense of performance, was a better bet than Blue, so he was working him over higher and more complex jumps and funny obstacles—through tunnels, through the house by way of the windows and so on, while he was using scent from the National Scent Company to work Blue on coon and to check him off deer and rabbits and such. Freddie was working George at 5'6", and he asked me if I'd hold a pole over my head to test him. George took that fine, sailed over as easily as most dogs do over the regulation heights the AKC sets—well, maybe not that easily, because there was now an agreeably ragged, but not raging, edge to the power he put into the big jumps, the sort that leads us to say an animal "soars," as if there were a moment when gravity grabbed, and the dog had to escape that, the same as when a plane takes off, and has to grab hard and hold to the air.

From a distance and at the right angle, George, because he was white and powerful, could fool you for half a second into thinking he was Jouster. I have it from Freddie that Jouster would sometimes look like George. A sudden glimpse of George could jolt me the way a sudden glimpse of Jouster would, if it hadn't always been me working Jouster. All power, that's what we would get a glimpse of. White is a misleading color, or maybe I mean that it's a leading one.

For the movie I dyed Jouster, shampooing in a tan dye and then brushing and spraying in the black, careful as hell around the eyes, so that Jouster was a regular black-and-tan. But even as a black-and-tan, he stood out like gem rock. Not that his inspection of the smell and texture gave him any reason to be pleased, but he still knew he was Jouster, despite the artificial smells on him.

It turned out that for the brave-dog-saves-boy-from-bear scene they needed a double for the boy, too, and the double couldn't be just furniture, had to be actually working consonantly and quietly with the dogs and the bear, and know how to read both, so, after talking to Freddie about it, I suggested that they use him.

They were, as usual, using food as a lure to the right behavior. In this case they kept the bear hungry, planning to release him from a cage that had no food in it to one he knew always had food in it, finding the right moment, of course, so that he would be sure to head for the food and not for the dog or the boy.

Jouster was to come in as the bear appeared to be getting to the boy, who would be on the ground, having stumbled and fallen running from the bear (this part would be filmed separately, later, so that it would match), and Jouster was to cross the scenery in a way that made it look as though he were deflecting the bear from the boy.

What I had to do was turn Jouster to me at the moment it looked (everyone hoped) as though the bear had started to go after Jouster but had in fact gotten revved up for the last stretch toward his bear-style kibbles. I wouldn't stop Jouster hard but would give a long, strong Whoa! so that what you would see in the movie would be a triumphant dog looking after his insolent but retreating enemy. There would also be close-ups, using the regular dog actor and boy actor, hugging each other with the boy doing that sort of half sobbing that in the movies means a relieved boy who knows the woods somewhat but tends to get into scrapes. We didn't need Jouster or Freddie for that, just for the shot of the dog deflecting the bear from the boy.

Sugar bears who aren't hungry and who are safely housed in sturdy cages can be quite chummy and even invent new and charming gestures of bear-and-person or bear-and-dog friendship. But I don't know what the people who work with them in the open are doing, and I can't tell what they think they are doing, either, but some of the handlers love the animals, they say, but they love the tigers and the jaguars and so on too. Wild-animal trainers seem sort of like collectors to me.

The morning we did that scene, I awakened to find Luke in the kitchen, scribbling. This was hardly the first time, but after our talk, the sight made me feel trembly for an instant, Luke looked so real, and I thought that maybe it was a waste to go off playing with bears for movies that couldn't be any good, anyway, on the off chance that someone would make a good movie and use my dog, and I thought of staying home, and dropping it all, and proposing to Luke that we get married. It was just a moment, but it was a full moment.

I made a plan. I would go to just teaching classes and training whatever came in, and Jouster would be a good dog to have for demonstrations, even if he couldn't be trusted with real work with the posse. Outside of working hours I would do whatever Luke wanted to do. I would save up for some decent furniture. I would buy him a writing desk to replace the shelves in the living room where I kept some training books and stuff that I hadn't read for years.

Luke looked up to greet me, and as he did, his hand moved over the manuscript, and I opened my mouth to propose to him but the moment was gone, replaced by childish frustration and what came out was, "If it's so private you can't let me even see what you're working on, then it's too private for my kitchen table!"

So much for my plan; I'd have to find another time to ask him to marry me. Anyway, Luke was shouting back, "Look, did you know that even when you aren't looking at them or listening to them that people go right on existing? What am I taking from you? Did you know that in inland Brazil at this very moment there is a mutant butterfly who is driving an otherwise quite peaceful cloud-backed boa insane? The butterfly, see, is teasing the boa. A boa should be able to take care of that so fast, the naturalist can't see it to record it in the journal, but this butterfly gives off a kind of odor that makes the muscles of any constrictor go all dreamy with love, and all the while the brain of the snake rages as usual. Did you know that? That we don't have a number small enough to indicate how much of the planet needs you or any one of us? That the planet gets on fine without you're even knowing about it? What's the deal? You don't want me to write?

Will you want to put me out in a run, too, like you did with Jouster when you got tired of him?"

"When he got too dangerous to have in the room at night, when I was too tired to wake quickly, when I had to choose between having him there or having you there, when I realized he was worthless!"

"Or in his case and mine, is the problem just that we don't fit into your fantasies well enough?"

"Then how can you . . ." Fortunately, perhaps, I didn't have time to finish, for what would I have said? *Anything*, at that point. *Anything at all.* I remembered that Freddie had wanted me to work out some problem with George as soon as I could, and we had a bit of time, so I turned and headed, blind, toward the kennels. I ran straight into George, bringing both of us down as he was returning from a retrieve over the hurdles. Several points there for George who, unlike a lot of dogs, didn't snap at me or chew but gave me some licks and went on to finish the exercise, to Freddie's delight.

Freddie, in fact, was exultant, grasping George's front paws and doing a sort of waltz. "Oh, ma'am, oh, thank you, I would never have thought of it, and if I had, I wouldn't have trusted my judgment and training to dare even to ask you about it. But you thought of it for me and did it."

I was rubbing an elbow that might turn out to be more than a little sore for a while. Time to get up off the ground, I decided. "Thought of what?"

"That way to test his steadiness. Now I know for sure there's a real dog here, and I see what you've been trying to tell me. I'm sorry if I'm not saying it the way you would, but you showed me. And he was there, he came through, he did his job for me, and he even managed to lick you on his way. That was pretty funny and smart of him."

Freddie had me. All I could think of to say was, "That's a pretty good triumph for him to quit on today. Besides, you and I have got to go bear huntin' "

"Thank you, ma'am."

I screeched, "Don't call me ma'am!" Freddie was still a little annoying about that kind of thing, but not annoying enough for shouting. I seemed to be shouting at everything this morning. He paused, confused for a bit, and looking almost sick at this change in his heroine, if Freddie could look sick, nervously holding the leash in a formal, obedience-trial loop. I hoped I could salvage his peace of mind after my jerky outburst, so I said, "We'll leave just before eight."

"Yes, uh . . . Miss Brannigan."

"Diane. Call me *Diane."*

"Yes, m—okay, Diane."

Just before we finished loading to go, Luke came out and tried to put his arm around me and wished me luck. I said, "Thank you," but went rigid, and he didn't go on, or else he couldn't, or else he hadn't meant anything in the first place but ordinary politeness.

Then he said, "Take care of Freddie and Jouster," and I felt his awkwardness as badly as I felt my own, or almost. I had never lived with polished wood, just varnished stuff.

So as usual these days I wasn't thinking, except to worry, and worry isn't thinking, worry keeps you holed up somewhere besides the present moment, the present of the moments. I kept seeing Luke's face, and what I wanted was to please him. I was scared because he was going, so I wanted to please him.

So I wasn't in the moment when the moment came. They had released the bear, Jouster was heading out fast. The bear was heading out, too, and do you know how fast a bear heads? But the bear hadn't read the script, and he headed, not for his food but straight in for Freddie, or almost; Freddie was almost in a line with the gate to the main compound, and it was probably some animal there the bear was after, or some animal's dinner. I wasn't thinking, just working on automatic, so with the timing off, I didn't say anything, like I had never held a leash.

Just for half a second I didn't say anything, just stood there woolgathering and missed my cue for that half second, which was long enough for Jouster to put himself ahead of the bear and jump him, the two of them rolling right toward Freddie, or was it the bear on top of Jouster at first? For half a second, half a century, I watched this and stayed still like a tourist. If I'd called him when I should, he would have gone right on by Freddie, or maybe I didn't have the control on him I thought, but either way I didn't belong where I was.

Freddie hadn't stayed still; the bear was on Jouster, so Freddie was on the bear, that fast, was pounding on the bear's skull, just above his eyes, with a skillet that was fortunately real iron, a prop for the scene, but it didn't slow the bear all that much from finding new ways to tear into Jouster, who was faster even than I had thought. Fast as Jouster was, he didn't know anything, and the bear was doing all right. Jouster had brains and speed, but the bear had weight, and even if he was declawed, he still had a mouth full of teeth and plenty of ursine agility. The bear was no longer a nondescript brown working bear; he was as rude and aboriginal as a white bear on the white top of the world instead of a courtier whose passions were contained to amuse the boudoirs of Hollywood palaces.

I've seen actors get into unscripted scenes with wild animals and come out with a brave showing once in a while, but this one would be a tough one to forget—that skinny, redheaded kid going in on top of that bear and yelling at him as if there was no more reason the bear should disobey him than that George or Blue should—"Damn bear! No-name bear! Leave our dog alone! You are just a stupid old bear, and it's about time you knew it." His voice was shrill but a real handler's voice for all that, though he shouldn't have gone in. He was hanging on to the top of the bear, it looked like, like a stick of a carrot-topped rodeo cowboy with one hand on the bear's ear, the other swinging the skillet.

Louie was ready with his weaponry—mainly a tiger hook and a tranq gun, a real one. He took aim, but Freddie was in there and Debbie had broken from her pose in the background and joined him. Debbie was Louie's, and just about everyone else's, favorite elephant. Debbie poked her trunk into the fracas, and you couldn't tell just what she was doing, but there was Freddie, suddenly separate from it all, staggering toward me, and he was something to hang on to, a weight once he realized he was out of the fight, but Debbie's trunk was still in there and she would have stepped on the bear, too, but she didn't.

Instead—I wouldn't swear to this—she seemed to be *tickling* the bear, who pretty soon let loose of Jouster. Then Debbie seemed—but maybe I don't want to think Jouster left even a hopeless fight—she seemed to eject Jouster, pushing him away from the bear in a graceful arc.

Louie was aiming again, but the bear suddenly remembered what he'd come out for in the first place and trundled nonchalantly over to the cage with the food, with an anxious Louie behind him, to lock the cage as soon as the bear had gone in.

The bear's name was Honeybee, I swear it.

Freddie's shoulder looked broken and was, it turned out, but a green-twig break and just this side of unbearably agonizing. He wasn't sure how or when that had happened; he thought the bear might have rolled over him at one point.

Jouster had come out of the fight and fallen, and I thought for a moment he was dead. There wasn't a twitch out of him. Maybe I had underestimated Debbie's talents in the sugar-bear tickling line, but I couldn't imagine anything short of death causing either of two such creatures to let go once a hold had been established. I didn't even feel, for a second or two, like bending over to find out; I was too sick about Freddie, who was obviously hurt, and who had gotten hurt in my keeping because I wasn't up to the keeping of anything, not being able to keep my mind off my worthless lover long enough to do a decent job of work.

Jouster roused himself then, groggy as though he were coming out of anesthesia at first, but pretty steady on his feet, on which he walked slowly back to me. He turned to show me his shoulder, which was torn across the bone. Apparently the bear wasn't that good at dog killing, since he missed the neck, or maybe Jouster was that fast. It looked ugly as hell, but he wasn't losing as much blood as he could have been, and he was fairly sprightly still, and his thick coat made it hard to tell. No trembling, his eyes okay, his gums still pink. He should have been in shock but wasn't, so there was quite a bit to him, screw loose or no.

The ambulance, which had been there automatically largely because the shooting was monitored, had Freddie scooped up and off to the hospital before I could think anything out except to wonder how that kid had stayed alive this long with that kind of crazy guts.

The director was out of his mind with joy. He had kept the cameras rolling.

Sixteen
JOUSTER'S
TEETH
AND
LUKE'S

The director got, as directors do, carried away with directing things around and ordered the drivers to take Freddie to Our Lady of the Hill, which is the best hospital around, but I intervened and insisted on Jurupa General because I knew I could get Dr. Sid, who is the best doctor around and a student of ours, to meet us there, and he did. Jouster's injury and Freddie's made me yearn for Sam as I was finishing formalities at the hospital in order to take Freddie and Jouster home.

Jouster had quite a slash from the bear's teeth, which I washed out at the hospital. It was slow, and the nurses there were aware that germs didn't leap off dogs as soon as they walked into an emergency room. Normally I wouldn't trust an M.D. with one of my dogs, but Dr. Sid had taken time to learn some veterinary medicine and stitched Jouster up, Jouster standing still for it, though it plainly hurt like blazes. We didn't have to knock him out. If he had been human, he would have clenched his teeth, turned red and sweated, but what he did was to stand there, trembling only slightly. He looked rumpled, with the dye now making his coat too stiff in places, and even crankier than the wound gave him a right to, with the smell of the dye still disgruntling him.

At home I showed the wound to Sam and went off to get some hydrogen peroxide, which we were unaccountably low on, or so I said, but it was because I felt like crying, and even Homer, who had cut short a duty round when we drove up and was licking a grateful Jouster, didn't stop the tears when he took a try at licking them off. When Freddie was gone, I let the tears go, and Sam had a fit.

"Goddammit, Diane, I don't know what's gotten into you about this dog, but I'd be willing to lay money that Slough probably did some of his screwy agitation routines with the dog and you didn't work to desensitize him because he took the pressure so beautifully for you, which ought to have told you that this dog might get overeager, but he doesn't make mistakes about who should get it. I'll bet you are so out of your senses, you didn't even see that Jouster wasn't going for that bear idly—did the director keep the cameras rolling?"

"Yeah."

"I have a hunch, Annie. You haven't worked much with bears. You might have been mooning over Luke, but I don't think it was your fault. You go in and insist to see the footage before they edit it. You weren't thinking, but it sounds to me like Jouster deflected the bear, not just from Freddie but from in general going on a rampage, and thank the gods for that elephant. I'm going to get hold of Slough and wring him like a washrag until we get the whole truth about this dog.

"Also, have you checked that left hind leg, because I swear

there's something there besides the shoulder, maybe just bruising, but let's find out. What is *wrong* with you? You taught *me*
how to see lameness. Look, I'll trot him out, you watch."

Sam did, and indeed Jouster was going short—taking a
shortened stride on the left hind. It wasn't all that easy to see,
since there was also that gash in the shoulder, but I should have
seen it. When you felt the leg over, the tenderness was unmistakably there, apparently just in the muscle, since it seemed more
sensitive to touch than to movement, and I had felt him over
and not seen it. We brought Jouster back into my cottage.

Sam said, "You stay put. I'm going to get hold of Slough."

"Sam! Slough didn't have anything to do with my screwing
up."

"I'm going to get the truth out of him."

He stopped and looked at me, then bent over and kissed
me, on the mouth, very tenderly. "I still owe you for putting the
brakes on when I got going messing things up because of the
dumb dog routines I picked up in 'Nam, which were nearly
brutal and therefore just right for my character defects. I'll call
from your kitchen if you want, if you'll make some fresh coffee."

I couldn't figure out what in the world good it would do for
Sam to call Jerry Slough, but at that moment that idea of Sam in
my kitchen, rampaging around while I made coffee, felt very
good to me.

What Sam meant by owing me was that the experience of
using dogs to do the kind of thing Zeus had done, finding that
valley, not that the other dogs did as well as Zeus, in 'Nam, had
blinded him. Using dogs for slaughter had left him with virtually
no ability to read a dog and find out what physical hurts were
making the work go wrong, or what false beliefs the dog held
that he had to be turned around on, and he tended to get
tougher on the dogs instead of thinking first about how best to
get tough, or when tough didn't do him a damn bit of good.

It had been the fear Sam tried to tell Luke about, sensing
the same thing in Luke, fear of too many consequences, making

Sam that way, but when he stopped being afraid, he turned out to have an eye so accurate, it made lasers look silly when it came to knowing what was wrong with a dog and fixing it fast, if there was any fast fixing possible. Sam thought I had done something for him, and maybe I had. It wasn't for him exactly, but for what I knew Sam saw in the dogs, and at the time I hadn't known that you could really be afraid of how well a dog can do, so what I'd done was, I just kept talking dog, maybe.

Oh, hell, Sam and I owe each other for everything.

He got hold of Slough and told him come to the kennel, and Slough said he wouldn't, but Sam did 't pause to argue because when Sam is mad and wants people to show up, they show up. While we waited, Sam brushed the grass and twigs out of my hair and put fungicide on a couple of cuts I had, and this seemed perfectly natural, like Homer licking Jouster, even though Sam and I didn't do that kind of thing much.

When Slough arrived, all Sam did was bring him in the house and say, "Now. Tell us about that dog." What he had to say was brief—he knew what Sam meant, knew Sam's opinion of his attack training. Yes, Jouster had been agitated to the point of all-out man-stopping.

And we didn't have to ask but did—no, Jouster hadn't had any obedience with it. Besides which, we knew that Jerry wouldn't have followed up much on the man work, wouldn't have driven the nail home. So Jouster's bites weren't even mixed-up Shepherd, they were just what I had taught Sam to look out for in a dog—false beliefs that can be corrected. It's simple as pie to correct them on a dog that already has as much obedience work as Jouster did—it takes a little time, but it works.

When Slough was done, Sam nodded at the door like someone in a Cagney flick, and out he went. Our relationship to him hadn't changed, and we still might want to buy a dog or two from time to time.

Freddie had been listening on the other side of the (open) bedroom door where he had been instructed to lie down with his shoulder and his gash, which was not quite as bad as Jouster's, thanks to Jouster and Debbie. Now he stuck his head in the door and said, "Miss Diane! I mean, Diane! I saw Jouster today. Didn't you see him? There he was, brave as always, and he works straight, does his job, he's not a quitter—he's all that stuff you said was important in Blue and George, especially Blue, only Blue has a Coonhound way, and Jouster has a Shepherd way."

Sam asked, "Right, but what is a Coonhound way?"

Freddie saw he had an audience. "Well, it's more up trees, and at night with a full moon or with flashlights." He stopped, thinking over his reading, trying to remember. "Or both, maybe.

"And a Shepherd way is more circling, keeping things in place, like Jouster arresting a suspect or herding sheep."

Sam said, "Then Jouster didn't read the book today. Because it's Lion who's the big-game dog, so it should have been Lion on the bear today."

Freddie, a bit doped up, took this quite seriously and said, "Well, a Shepherd steps in, really, sir, that's what a Shepherd does. Steps in when the sheep go haywire, steps in when citizens go haywire and become criminals, and today Jouster stepped in when your Airedale went haywire by not being there. Do you know what I mean?"

A Shepherd steps in. It wasn't bad, and Sam and I started giggling, because Sam had seen me as I listened to Slough, and we said, yes, Freddie, we knew, we both knew. Then I decided to give him a hard time and said, "Okay, kid, did you notice how *I* blew it today?"

"You! No, Diane, you wouldn't do any such thing."

"Well, if I am incapable of blowing it, I am incapable of being wrong in my judgment of a dog, and you are guilty of a contradiction, and contradictions are something a trainer can't afford. Paradoxes are okay . . ." I started to say what a teacher had said once about a poem, then decided to drop it. "But contradictions are low-level, and you—"

Freddie didn't care. He interrupted and said, "And a Samoyed makes remarks, if he happens by, so you can laugh."

I couldn't go on, Sam and I were giggling so much. It was a decisive moment for Freddie, his full graduation if he got it right. His lower lip had started to shake just a little in the face of the cruelty of Sam and me giggling, but he got it right.

"Yes, I see, you judged Jouster to be fine in the first place, and you can't be wrong, by definition, like in mathematics, but on the other hand, then you judged him not to be fine, so that makes you contradictory, and now you are . . ." He thought it over. "Now you are in need of a Samoyed." Here, of course, he just started giggling with us, trying to control it because it hurt.

Then he thought up a good exit line, went to the door and turned to say it (he would have been wagging his tail so hard, he could hardly have stood if he were a dog, he was that pleased with it, overplaying it naturally). "I have to go check on George, *ma'am*. George just giggles all the time, there must be some more contradictions we don't know about. Could be the dog is a goner." And he turned and left but couldn't control a little burst of glee at having come up with that to say. He's going to be a terrific class instructor, is Freddie Kubie.

Then, at the same time, Luke got back from researching whatever feature he was on just as Sam picked up the telephone again, this time to call Dave and see what word there was on the Olsen case. Dave keeps working on a case like that.

Luke was plainly bursting with news, but he was quiet in the face of Sam's determination to make the phone call to Dave Buckman, which was only accidentally, I think, connected with what was going on just then. It was as if he woke up with this determination, the kind that makes whole biographies shift on their haunches. If I had heard Luke's news, been able to hear it . . . ? No. The details might have been different, but Luke still didn't know what had happened when I turned from Jouster, the night with Slough, the day in Joshua Tree.

And everyone's biography shifted that day on the fulcrum of how deeply Jouster meant what he said.

■

This was when Dave reported on the Olsen case. The child hadn't been kidnapped at all. Chuck Olsen had staged the whole thing to get the money out of his father-in-law, so all Jouster had done was exactly what I asked him to do—finger the criminal. Olsen's wife hadn't known what was going on, so he'd terrified her about her little girl, and he'd left his daughter with his girlfriend out in a motel out beyond Twentynine Palms, and the child hadn't known the woman before and wasn't in very good shape, apparently. Dave figured Jouster had been a lot too gentle with him.

"But," Dave said, "he did exactly what we asked him to do. That dog is going to come in handy again, I'll bet. And after this case, we won't have any trouble getting any judge anywhere to accept his evidence."

"That's all he was doing," I said to Luke after Dave hung up. "Just what I asked him to do!"

"But how did he know?"

"Probably the same way the detective knew, a hunch, except Jouster's knowledge is faster than ours, more accurate."

"But he couldn't even have known it was a kidnapping!"

"He just needed to know what didn't belong. I don't remember exactly what Olsen was doing or saying, but it didn't belong."

"Olsen must have been afraid and Jouster smelled his fear."

Sam said, "It's what Diane said, Luke. Fast knowledge. Jouster knew, that's all. Something to do with smell, maybe—but not fear. If dogs worried about fear, they'd be biting most people most of the time, probably. And something to do with Olsen's way of talking to Diane, Dave, the cops.

"But that doesn't account for it. It's something else, something that didn't fit. Homer would probably have known it, too, only he's had formal work transporting suspects, so he wouldn't have bitten. Next time Jouster won't bite, either, he'll have more formal education for his knowledge. The detective knew something didn't fit, too, but he knew it slower."

Luke said, "You're talking as though dogs had a direct line to God or something. That doesn't explain anything."

Sam said, "I don't know about God, but what Jouster knew, what dogs know, what you know if you know dogs—I guess it isn't exactly secular knowledge."

A detective on the case had become supicious of Olsen, who wasn't very good at sustaining his lies, although better than most, the cops said. Anyway, a lie detector backed up the detective, and both the detective and the machine backed up Jouster.

Not even Sam had thought Jouster might have been that right, or at least Sam hadn't said it out loud, but Jouster had been, and I had been right in the first instant I came to and recognized him, after my romantic trance that evening with Luke. And Sam was right that the problem wasn't a screw loose, at least not in Jouster's head—and there wasn't any problem now about working him to be reliable around weirded-out Hollywood types.

There was a problem—my not having any movie and therefore any weirded-out Hollywood types to work with.

Then Homer did a curious thing. He went over to stand beside Jouster and leaned sideways, gently, so that Jouster took a few steps sideways—Homer didn't lean against the sore shoulder, but he kept leaning until Jouster was standing next to me. Homer stationed himself in front of us both, in a caretaker stance, and Jouster leaned slightly on me with his head in that aggravating and, at that point, moving Shepherd way. Jouster wasn't exactly cooperating with Homer, and Homer was unlikely to be trying to further Jouster's career, as I explained to Luke later, but they were holding me up so that I didn't melt out of the kind of emotion you leave the movie theater with, or ought to. I melted, anyway. I had been right the first time about Jouster.

■

After a week or two, Jouster was pretty close to healed, the dye completely scrubbed out, and Luke asked me when I was going to start working him again. I saw no reason to just then, being still in need of a rest, meaning only a full day's work at the kennel and nothing new and exciting going on, but the thought of the movie, the way it could have been, whispered to me from time to time.

It whispered to Sam too. Sam inherited from somewhere a nice, though small, talent for drawing, and he made a few sketches for me of Jouster, with all of Alaska and North American/Oriental commerce in brutality suggested in the background, in street scenes. There was one right out of *The Call of the Wild,* with Frenchie clubbing a dog coming out of a crate, other rough types around, and dogs, and Jouster in the foreground, knowing everything and something else too.

Sam said that he had at least gotten that much out of our troubles, the need to draw the pictures—the pictures were real portraits of Jouster. You couldn't look at them and doubt who Jouster was, but even they didn't make me want to work Jouster just yet. The kennel had to be put back together, and so did my knowledge. It was restored but needed piecing back together, I told Luke.

Luke kept on about that, and I kept on him, too, saying terrible things about everything he didn't know about dog training. Luke, I suppose, wanted to make up for the past by encouraging me, but it came out as nagging. I wanted to be sure that never, never again would I turn from a dog like Jouster, but it came out as criticism of Luke. He started contradicting himself, and so did I, saying one day that I still couldn't be sure that

Jouster's attack response could be put permanently on safety, honest dog though he was, and then after Luke said something, I said that I didn't want to strain his shoulder, and then I agreed that a little jumping would probably be beneficial at this point, low jumps set on even grass, and Luke got on to *that* one. He was going a little crazy, I don't think he realized yet that he was bound to be crazy around me and Sam, so that was making him crazy. Or, he realized, we all realized but *didn't* realize, that Luke would never get any rest from his need to *do* something about the center of life at the kennel, or me, and the only thing to do was to leave it alone, so he was going to behave badly, and so was I.

On one particuarly hot day he shouted at me that I hadn't really had all my knowledge restored to me, or maybe I'd never had any. He really said that, with Jouster listening too. Luke said, "All right, all right, then. Damn it, Diane, make up your mind. I thought the heart was where honesty was stored, and all of us here have hearts, including especially me. *I'll* train him if you're too tired or chicken."

I shrugged and said, "You play with Jouster all you like. I've got to feed Homer." It didn't dawn on me that he would do anything. Luke walked into the equipment porch, got Jouster's collar and leash and Jouster, and said, "I'm going to *work* Jouster. Someone has got to, there's too much at stake!" Maybe if I had asked him what he meant then, maybe if I had paid attention to the book, to what Luke had been trying to say, maybe if . . .

I don't know why I just walked away, with an inquisitive Homer at my heels, letting Luke do that. I don't know why Luke had the idea to begin with. I don't know why I agreed. What I said was, "Fine. Just don't tell me about it."

Luke said, "I sure won't! Let Jouster do it if you ever want to know."

The next part is harder to tell. I was tired that evening, but I couldn't sit still in the house while anyone at all was messing with Jouster, so Homer and I strolled outside to watch. We didn't actually go in the gates of the training area but watched through the chain link although the gates were wide open.

What I had done was inexcusable, letting Luke take Jouster's leash, but not what Luke did, because he wasn't a dog trainer yet, not until a bit over an hour later, when Jouster made him into one, or at least gave him a glimpse.

During that hour Luke worked Jouster at top speed. I hadn't told him much about transferring a leash, but he was pretty good at getting it intuitively, except for the speed and pressure, and he took him over to the blacktop in that heat, being in too much of a rush to set up the other jumps in the grassy areas.

Jouster had had a hard time, even for him, and was educated in the rights and privileges of dogs who have had a hard time, who are hot and injured on top of that, and who are suddenly being asked to work with unwarranted intimacy with someone who had never even held his leash before, member of the family though he was, and there wasn't any reason for all of this as far as Jouster could see.

Luke took off the lead, which made my blood boil, as he didn't put a light line on the dog and worked him on retrieving over the hurdles, and doing this with no check line with a strange dog is a pretty basic sort of mistake to make—it was something Luke knew better than to do, but only in a theoretical sort of way. Luke knew a great deal, but he didn't know how authority can dangerously increase the scope and reach of word and gesture. Homer, who had seen a lot of dog training go on, watched Luke in amazement. Homer's amazement seemed to be, not so much at the actual mistakes being made but that it was *Luke* making them. There was Homer, jumping up anxiously, whining and watching over the top.

I hope that was the last time I ignore a dog as good as Homer, but six months earlier I would have been unable to imagine any concatenation of circumstances that would have led to any portion of the drama now taking place in my kennel, with me silently participating. That's what love does to you, or to me at least—

When Homer jumped up and put his paws on the chain link, his shoulders came higher than my head. He was looking down at me both figuratively and literally, asking me to do something to stop what was going on, but I was no more a dog trainer at that moment than Luke was, because I didn't stop it, even though I knew what had to be coming.

Instead of being a dog trainer, I was a woman pleading with the universe—it was no good pleading with Luke—not to let my man do this, set off in me this turning-away-and-not-turning-back. Maybe I had read Jack London too closely, so instead of just barking out a single command that would put a stop to it, I superstitiously prayed for Luke to *get it* in time and stop.

Luke wasn't putting as much pressure on Jouster as he'd seen me do, but Luke's mere picking up the leash was pressure for him, and Luke had no feel for the thresholds beyond which the dog does not allow your authority to go on a given day or at a given moment.

Of course, not all dogs are as clear about this as Jouster—I saw now that becoming very precise about the threshold was part of how he stayed relatively sane with the weird handling he had had—but clear or not, the threshold is as sharp in every case, it's just that some dogs aren't as sharp about letting you know exactly when you've reached it. There are dogs you could literally work to death, but Jouster wasn't one of them, not without love in it, like Buck pulling that damn sled out of the ice because Thornton had made a drunken bet.

Thornton won. I didn't.

What happened was fast and simple. Luke said, "Jouster, fetch!" Jouster refused. Luke started to correct him for his refusal, and Jouster bit him, a medium-sized bite, not much to what I took from Lion and one or two others but worth a trip to the emergency room for all that. He stopped bitting the instant the suddenness of the pain made Luke stagger back and stumble.

What he had wanted was to get Luke off his back, then he quit. Luke was as safe with him now as a newborn lamb with a good sheepdog.

Homer was down from the fence at once, punching it so hard that the force of his dense weight pushing against it made the whole length of it shudder as though the fence itself were wincing away from what had gone on in its enclosure.

Homer is too long to corner easily or fast—he's built for serious landscapes—so it took him a moment to scramble around the gate, but once inside, he covered the distance between himself and Luke in what seemed to be a single, long, easy stride.

I thought Homer was going to go for Jouster the way he one time picked up a full-grown Malamute by the scruff of the neck—the Malamute was climbing up the leash, going for the twelve-year-old handler's throat—and carried the Malamute off to a corner, carrying and dragging and shaking him hard.

In this case, Homer planted himself between Luke and Jouster like a referee, looking from one to the other, checking that they would stay separated, not that Luke was dashing back for the dumbbell and the line of command. Then, satisfied that Jouster was rational, Homer walked back to check out Luke's wound—demanded to see it, actually, licked enough to find out how bad it was—and then turned back to Jouster and whined at him urgently as he stood still for Homer to examine *him* for injuries.

That's when I really tumbled to it. Homer was never wrong about the justice of a dog/human tangle, and Homer was honoring the justice of Jouster's move.

Freddie and Sam had been right all along, and so had Jouster, attack training or no attack training. So I learned it yet again, the lesson I spend my life learning: The dog is the ultimate authority. Always, because even when the dog is wrong, it turns out that there isn't any other authority. Like Sam out in the jungle with Zeus.

I saw and thought all of this and much more in the one and three-quarters seconds it took me to catch up with Homer. Such thinking doesn't occur in anything you'd want to call *time,* and there was Luke to deal with.

Luke had learned the same things, perhaps—some knowledge blazed in his face. He had also learned a false lesson with it, about humiliation, and we usually learned such lessons whether we want to or not, but virtually no one learns all of the right ones, and almost everybody starts by learning the false ones.

Luke was sweating heavily, between the heat and his wound, though he looked as though the pain from the bite had already settled down to a fairly steady roar; dog bites do that, reach their depth fast and then stay there, humming one of the longest songs of damage known to nature. The first time you hear the song, it is a bitter-sounding one, though it modulates later. I guess Luke was listening to it for the first time, hence the wrong lesson about humiliation.

Hence also his saying, "I see, Di, I really see. I didn't see it when you got hurt, but I see now."

He didn't see a damn thing. What I wanted to say was . . . I wanted to say I loved him, had wanted him to know.

What I said was, "Come on, let's go get that thing stitched up."

"I should have listened to you."

"Could have, maybe. You can't anymore, because I'm joining a cloister, taking a vow of enough silence to go with my damn ignorance. Look at Homer and Jouster." Freddie had arrived and was standing by Homer, Blue hanging back a little behind him. "'Look at Jouster and Homer."

Homer towers over Jouster the way Jouster towers over a Miniature Spaniel, but they looked to be the same size then, perhaps because both of us were on the ground being regarded gravely by the Shepherd and the Wolfhound. Homer was saying it all with his bearing, the way a king for whose sake his kind still existed did, though the kings no longer say it. When Homer says something silently like that, he forever changes the shape of silence.

I had forgotten for close to five minutes that I no longer had a lover. Now I thought that soon I should let Luke know that I knew and that it was okay. I thought of those months when I barely noticed that Luke was there, or that anything but Jouster and the movie and the reasons for Jouster and the movie existed. The movie no longer mattered because it was off, but I hadn't changed.

I tried to think how a man like Luke could love a woman who could talk about something besides her own crazy-kid dreams about movies. I remembered the rosewood table part of Luke's story, and in a way that was all I heard, even though the table was incidental to the riots, and to writing, meaning. I looked down at his hand—no bites are pretty, but for me, dog bites, even when they don't tear, pack more ugliness for the size and seriousness of the wound than most other violations of the skin, and this one looked outrageous, an offense against Luke's beauty and an emblem of what happens when dolts of dog trainers go haring off after perfection.

Then I said, "No, Luke, no shame, no shame." I muttered that and tried to say that that's what Homer and Jouster were saying; dogs say it with posture. Sam had arrived, read things and rearrived with the car pulled up outside the gate, so I talked to myself, mute before a memory of Luke writing, writing.

Everyone was in the training area now, Prince first, as proud and as dainty as ever, probing Luke for soundness where even Homer would have been too gawky, then that strange and beautiful Lion with Sam. Luke was talking too much. He was talking to me, but I had gone into a flimsy state of being, hearing nothing. I was realizing that Jouster could probably act this scene and that it might be a way, with the bite next to the

dog leaping like a thought of God's, to film what you're supposed to be honoring when you work a dog, and how much, if
not what, is at stake. Because dogs and people are what they
are, and the universe is the way it is, a dog biting a handler is a
long song of damage, like the light turning on itself. Dogs don't
"turn on their masters," but the light turns on itself if you aren't
respectful.

Sam was, as usual, standing there quietly, like the northern
lights, so I filled him in. He just nodded, the way he does, and
said, "Well, we've still got to hunt up a vet or something for that
untidiness you've got there. Vet'll sew it up, won't make us
quarantine Jouster, save you from having a messy scar into the
bargain."

This reminded Luke that he was enough of a city boy to
want a real doctor working on his own actual flesh-and-blood
self, and he said so, then winced, the excitement of talking
having made him move his arm.

But Luke was trainer enough to remember to call to Jouster,
who may have known that he was right while he was in action,
but for a Shepherd, that's different from standing there contem-
plating a brother-become-fallen enemy. Jouster's forehead
looked less sculptured, with worry lines wrinkling it. He hesitated, and Luke called to him again and he walked up to him.
No cringing, walking into what might be punishment, prepared
to do whatever he had to do, take what he had to take. He
sniffed at the underside of the hurt arm, and a couple of drops
of blood fell on his forehead.

Homer hesitated, standing back and almost receding from
the scene, the way the gigantic Irish heroes receded from Ire-
land. But when he saw Luke reach down to caress Jouster lightly,
Homer breathed again and let go of the tension, now that it
looked as though the rest of us were going to avoid being idiots
for a while at least—Wolfhounds are too ancient to expect much
more than from the most stable of humans.

Homer walked over to Luke as well, reminding me that the

walk of a good Wolfhound is designed for a more stately time, and when he reached Luke and Jouster, he cleaned up Luke's blood from Jouster's forehead.

Luke was apologizing again, talking about the dead now, saying, "I'm sorry, Jouster. I wanted to make myself dead, only what I said was safe. I sat with Esther's corpse for hours and didn't learn a damn thing."

I thought but didn't say, "Don't listen to Jouster's corpse. Listen to Jouster." It was a prayer. But I was afraid Luke wouldn't give up his corpses, maybe they were his subject, and there wasn't time for corpses at our kennel. My love for Luke became something fixed. He had messed up with my dog, I had *let* him mess with my dog. Luke was lovely, but he wasn't my loveliness.

I had to talk to Sam. Luke was lovely, but he had messed with my dog, and I had to talk to Sam. So after I got Luke back from the hospital—he was tired and just wanted to sleep—I called Sam over. I would have gone to his cottage, but I figured I ought to be around in case Luke awoke, needing something.

Sam had seen the same thing I had, a movie with a scene something like the one we had just lived through. We didn't talk about Luke but about how it might be a scene in a movie about the beginning of Scotland Yard, with the hero learning what dogs were. We talked about how the jump would have to be a bit higher than the one Jouster had been jumping, and how high it should go, and how the movie would be about the knowledge of dogs and how that's the knowledge of knowledge itself, boundless, bounding out of the natural.

Sam said, "And about how you don't get tired of it. Maybe a movie about a dog business instead, about the people who don't get tired of it."

Sam and I looked at each other, each of us wondering which one was going to say the new thing that we hadn't said before, because you do get tired. He had gotten—well, call it tired—in Vietnam, and when Zeus died, wanting comfort instead of truth, and I had gotten tired.

Sam said, "Lion is white when the light's on her just right and she's moving."

"Yeah. So's Homer. It's a good thing most dogs go around disguised most of the time."

"The First Commandment was probably just, 'Thou shalt not get tired of the light,' " Sam mused, reaching for it, "Only people need explanations, so Moses disguised the light as 'the Lord thy God.' " The rest was kennel rules.

"And, Annie, Luke does see. But his way of living it isn't yours. He's never going to get it about these kennel rules."

"I tried to find a way to honor his kennel rules."

"That's his job, Annie. You went and got yourself Jouster, who isn't disguised."

"That's right, and dog trainers never get tired. But there should be something in the movie about what the partner has to do when the trainer gets tired anyway."

Seventeen
JOUSTER

The next morning Luke woke early because both the dope they had given him at the hospital and sleep had worn off, and his arm was hurting. I gave him more dope, and he fell back into a heavy sleep with nothing to say.

I went over to see Sam, and I started trying to tell Sam the whole thing, which Sam knew. Until Luke, we had both kept our love lives pretty well out of the kennel, I said, and Sam said that we hadn't, not really, at least he hadn't.

"What was the matter with us?" Sam said. "Do you know what I would do? I would say, 'If only there were a woman like Annie.' "

I remembered the night, eight and a half years ago, when he'd suggested wine and I had backed off because I didn't want to lose his friendship, knowing as I said it what he was about to say, which was that he hadn't pressed it for the same reason.

But it was important that it get said right about Luke. I wanted to talk about everything about Luke that didn't show up in his discomfort. What I said didn't come out the way I expected. All I remember saying is, "Sam. There's nothing *wrong* with Luke. *Nothing* wrong with him! He just gets a little silly sometimes, but not so often as I do and . . ."

Sam said, "There's nothing wrong with you, either." I looked at Sam and thought for a second that he was going to break down and wondered how things were going with him.

Then his face composed itself—we were across the kitchen table from each other, the way we are when we talk or make plans—and Sam said, "Come on into the living room and lean back a little. Did you sleep?"

I hadn't much. I said so and followed Sam obediently. Lion got off his chair and waited for him to settle in it, but he sat on the couch instead and looked up at me, and his face looked the way it does when he's buckling on a harness or sizing up a dog or working one—it looked competent, and he held his hand out to me and said, "There's nothing wrong with Luke. I tried to tell myself different, but that's nothing cotton-candy about him. If we'd seen that, he wouldn't have gotten hurt. We should have known he had to act."

"But there is *nothing wrong with you.*"

I sat down next to him, and he added, "There's nothing wrong with us, either."

I cried a while, and fell asleep on Sam's shoulder, and was weightless while the sun moved and no dogs were worked.

After three or four days, Luke got back to writing, using his left hand on a small portable typewriter—and it wasn't until then that I *heard* him, belatedly, when he had been saying he wanted to write. I had heard him saying, "I want to write but can't because it's too dangerous," and okay he had been saying that, like I'd said things, but he'd also wanted to write the way I had wanted Jouster. There he was, wincing and trying to support his right arm—Jouster had bitten his writing arm—on pillows and tapping away with two fingers from his left hand. When he felt better, he moved his typewriter and a change of clothes back up to the place in Oak Glen, saying he had to think, and first he had to write, and that he would be back, and it wasn't until after he left that I learned from Sam that he had seen me bawling on Sam's shoulder and had drawn conclusions.

I started to bawl about Luke half a dozen times a day, that was my body being nostalgic, but I didn't call him, I didn't want to know what he would say and figured he was right to get out, and even if I wasn't constantly praying for my body to get it that I had made a choice, and so had Luke, there had been that about the way he was writing that had something to do with his kennel rules, and that was something to leave alone. *Leave it alone,* I had to say to myself over and over again, but I didn't lose sight of Jouster.

And Sam's shoulder—no, Sam, continued to be there, only now he was chatty. He bragged about Lion and talked about Zeus without that hard look of someone who can't stand to have his story misunderstood, in the almost happy way one can get to in time, remembering a great dog, even if there never comes a time when you can say the dog's name without summoning some insubstantial residue of motion away from you, but Sam let that come and go and invented new languages for new stories of Zeus. Zeus was dead, but Sam wasn't, and there wasn't anything deadly about Lion these days, though I couldn't answer for her if someone like Olsen were to show up.

He said one time, "A movie about Zeus, or Lion, would have to be black-and-white; color would distract from what Zeus was working on, traces of light in the jungle." And that was one of the times of small blessing; Luke wasn't there to ask about all the people who had been killed. I imagined that he was there and did ask and that I then said, "Why do you think it has to be art?"

What I said to Sam was, "Yes, in a movie, the only consequence of a dog's power is truth."

Sam said, "Almost the only consequence. Look what's been going on around this kennel, at least half of it for a movie. Power is inconvenient no matter what you do. Look at Lion," he added, laughing as Lion stood up under the coffee table, lifting it before crouching back and extricating herself.

Lion had gotten up because it was time for her to patrol the house, check out of the windows. Before doing this, she stopped to lay her boxlike Airedale-hound jaw on Sam's knee.

"Yeah, while we're at it, look at Lion," I said.

Then I thought, Luke's writing. Maybe he knows now. Maybe he's not tired anymore.

■

In the period before the trial, while Olsen was still out on bail, I asked him if I could work on Jouster's steadiness around him, because Jouster needed that kind of work. Olsen agreed because Dave said it would make Jouster friendlier toward him in court, that he would look less awful to the jury if Jouster didn't bristle at him, which was true, but it was mostly Dave backing me up on the dog. I had Jouster stand-stay while Olsen stroked him, and I don't have the language to tell you about the faces that man made while he was doing it. The first time Jouster's bristles stiffened, but he didn't move. Probably never would have, but it was good to be sure. And I went down and worked Jouster on the honor farm, too, the minimum-security prison that a friend of mine was personnel manager of, to make sure he understood that just because someone was sullen didn't mean he should act right off.

One morning almost a month later, Luke called and said he wanted to come over and show me something.

Thirty-seven minutes later he was there—I had been watching the clock. I had such notions as getting Sam's trousers out of sight, but all I did was sit there, hoping he had a new woman.

Luke walked in the kitchen with Prince, giving only perfunctory recogniton to the greeting they got from Homer and Jouster, although Prince performed several trapeze acts of joy.

And Luke opened with this: "You are the worst excuse for a research assistant I ever saw, and you are supposed to know dogs, but instead, since you wouldn't damn talk to me about Jouster, I had to talk to Kaye. And Sam. For a while I talked to Sam. For a while Sam and I talked about dogs and movies a lot while you were working Jouster. So now if you can stay fairly calm for two or three months, maybe four, we're going to be working together on that movie if they'll let me in as a consultant. Not the movie you wanted. Not Jack London." Luke wasn't telling this very well. "Because you *would* keep talking to me about how it was hard to see white on white, or as Sam put it, you were so used to seeing white on white, you didn't know what I was asking, that white dogs in white snow were only a f'rinstance, but I couldn't forget that image, dog on snow, so you have actually proved it can be done with Jouster, and now I'm going to prove it again, big, and you and Sam have got to help, because I have to write the script from my own fiction."

"Aren't you going to say something about our relationship and what the hell you are talking about?"

"No! I had to talk to Jack Kaye because you wouldn't talk to me. And then I had to be polite to the producer, who is okay, a young guy, smart. He listened to Kaye. He wants to do the movie, but only if you are head trainer, and he's got a dog he wants to train with you so he'll understand his role better, and—"

"Who wants to work . . . *what* dog?"

"The lead, Tony Boucher, and the producer insists on it too—"

"What breed of dog?"

"If you can find it, a German Shepherd. Black-and-tan, German breeding. So that he can have one, he's always wanted one, and he figures it's time now, so that he will understand Jouster better on camera.'"

"Okay. That *might* work, if it's the right dog, even with an actor, but he might not be ready for what it is he's 'always wanted.' I'll do it if he's committed to training the dog, and he might have to go through some tough times." I didn't notice that Luke talked as though he knew something about German lines.

"*And* of course only if all of this comes off that I wasn't going to tell you about until I finished, and I still can't tell if the story is any good, but the producer likes it and maybe it's good."

"Story?" This was stupid of me, but Luke was so full of forward motion, everyone could be stupid.

"The one I told you about, the one I've been working on ever since that night I told you about the riots at Isla Vista, ever since the first time I saw Jouster and you told me so that I started to see. The story, the first of the stories, novels, I always wanted to write and chickened out on because novels were too long and too chancy, and when I was a kid, it used to have King Arthur and Merlin and knights in it. I only learned some other versions recently.

"It was clinched, ready to finish, when I talked with Kaye the time he told me about Jouster biting him—nipping him, really—and how you and Jouster just turned him around that day in his suite, and he's been sober ever since and is back with his old lover, who only left him because of the booze."

"Hell, that day the only ones in this state that had any faith were Jouster and Pierre," I said. "You remember, all I could say was that Jouster was trash. You can't count on a dog trainer that thinks like that, and anyway, what's so noble about biting a poor old drunk? Luke."

"It's one way of taking a drunk seriously, I suppose, and anyway, the 'poor old drunk' paid better attention to Jouster than you did that day." He paused and added, "I had the novel finished, a draft, anyway, the day Jouster bit me, and I was angry because you and Sam didn't listen to my news. I had written the book, so I thought I knew." He said this absentmindedly as he left the room and the porch to go back outside to his car, as though it didn't matter, the way chitchat doesn't matter. This was news, but it wasn't *the* news.

Then he was back with a typescript and still babbling. I suddenly realized that writers have to babble sometimes, and so do dog trainers, though not so much. "Here!" He handed me a real bundle of papers, all nicely jogged and in a box. His face looked radiant in a new way—you would have thought he was carrying the grail back to the home palace, not that the kennel was the palace of Luke's grail.

The first sheet of paper had only a title and a byline, like this:

Jouster:
The Story of a Dog
by
Luke Zeller

I turned over the title page and saw that there was an epigraph there that could break your heart if you were into that sort of thing. It was said for Yeats to write, but joyful for Luke. Me, too, now. It went:

> . . . *Now that my ladder's gone*
> *I must lie down where all the ladders start*
> *In the foul rag and bone shop of the heart.*

I thought of how a dog trainer is like a deaf-mute: they can't say anything, they can only know. And I thought about how a writer is like a deaf-mute too. Luke babbled because his was also the knowledge that can't say anything.

■

But his book spoke, spoke to me and to just about everybody, judging by the reviews, spoke about the power in every creature human and otherwise, just the way Luke had wanted his writing to do, and Jouster and the world are answering now, because we're making that movie. Luke had written a novel about a kid about Freddie's age, who gets a dog like Jouster, only the kid was more like Luke than Freddie, and what Luke had been doing in Oak Glen was changing the book to have a bite scene in it, pretty much like the real one where Jouster bit Luke. Luke's a real writer; you can see when he tells it that the bite is everything and nothing, the way Zeus finding that valley of Vietcong was everything and nothing, the way love affairs and turning Jouster away from the door and getting it right and getting it wrong are everything and nothing. They are nothing because the light is everything, what we can see most of the time are just details on the surface of the light, but the details are everything for us. Everything, because even with a book and a movie it's hard to see white on white, which is what I thought I knew but didn't.

After I read the book several times, one time when Luke and I were talking about the script where it had to be changed, and Luke needed to know what could be filmed and what couldn't with Jouster, I said to Luke now that he had the book, he would know, and he could just give it to people in his life and then they would know; dog bites and broken hearts weren't required anymore.

Luke said that I didn't get it, but looking at his face, I did. His face, like his heart, wasn't broken at all, it was rearranged by knowledge, and that's when I found out that once in a while for a moment there can be too much beauty. "Everything is as it should be," he said. "Everything is already in place." After the film, he said, he was going back to San Francisco.

I spent a while figuring out how to ask Sam to marry me, because I wanted everything to be just right. Maybe after the last day of shooting, I thought, or on one of those afternoons when we went inside to make love and usually forgot to unplug the kennel phone. Anyway, I waited too long, and one day Sam just said, "Annie, it's time," and a couple of days after that we got out our good shoes and went over to City Hall and went public.

Like all real stories, this one goes on, but that is all I'm going to tell you anything about, except that Sam and I are studying marriage—there is more to it than you might think, and less, because Sam and I should have gotten married nine years ago, but how could we have? What did we know? And Jouster and Homer are undiminished. No one is diminished.

In the script, Luke added a movie within the movie, *The Call of the Wild,* with George playing Buck. He did this just for Freddie, of course, but he's skillful and he made it look like the movie was missing on two cylinders without that, like the movie wasn't going anywhere without a witty Samoyed, so the producer went for it, and Freddie has his own contract.

Lion, of course, still breathes smoke and fire, which is natural to a dog whose ancestors had to stay on long, dark trails and repel the more vicious songs scattered by late lights and later darkness. Sam came right down hard on that dog, got to her, so now she gets to Sam, too, doesn't touch him, just flames for him. That fire cleaned Sam out so clean you could take it for love, which it is. That's how gentle she is with Sam, that's how *gentle.*

As for the real Jouster, he makes his character show up in that film, white on white or no. This is the end of my telling. I heard a director telling our director that it wouldn't work, the movie *Jouster,* because the modern thing to do with a dog story is to kill the dog off about halfway through so that everyone can learn compassion, but I'm not compassionate enough to kill off Jouster just yet, and his name is still there for anyone who wants to read it, because in the movie the dog has papers, and there, written down, is his name, Heaven's Jouster, so I have reached the beginning at last. We found the right dog and we have reached the beginning.